MANATEE BAY: RETREAT

Treasure Seeker Series - Book 1

AMY RAFFERTY

© **Copyright 2022 <Amy Rafferty>** — **All rights reserved.**

This is a work of fiction. Names, characters, places, and incidents either are products of the author's imagination or are used fictitiously. Any similarity to actual events or locales or persons, living or dead, is entirely coincidental.

All rights reserved. No part of this publication may be reproduced, stored in, or introduced into a retrieval system, or transmitted, in any form, or by any means (electronic, mechanical, photocopying, recording, or otherwise) without the prior written permission of the copyright owner.

The author acknowledges the trademarked status and trademark owners of various products referenced in this work of fiction, which have been used without permission.

The publication / use of the trademarks is not authorized, associated with, or sponsored by the trademark owners.

STAY UPDATED WITH ME

Thank you so much for purchasing or downloading my book! I am grateful to all my amazing readers.

To stay updated on all my latest books, newsletters, freebies and beautiful photos from the fabulous locations I write about, why not join my VIP group?

I will send you regular pictures of La Jolla Cove, San Diego and the Florida Gulf Beaches where I try to spend as much time as I can. I live in San Diego, my own 'Garden Of Eden' and I am in love with the sea and the beaches in the area. They inspire me to write lots of beachy mystery romance fiction to share with my awesome readers like you. To join me go to https://landing.mailerlite.com/webforms/landing/y6w2d2

You will be asked for your email. You also get a FREE BOOK whenever you sign-up!

FREE BOOK

To get your FREE copy of Cody Bay Inn Prequel - Nantucket Calling go to www.amazon.com/B0992NFTY1

FAMILY TREES

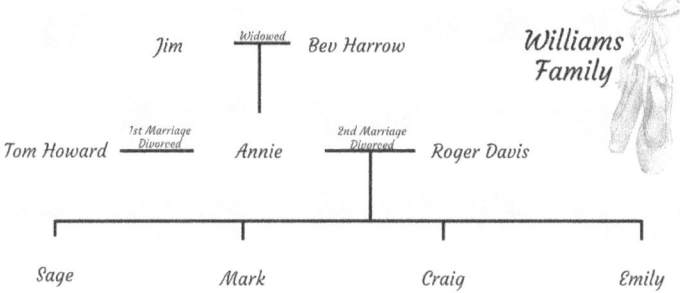

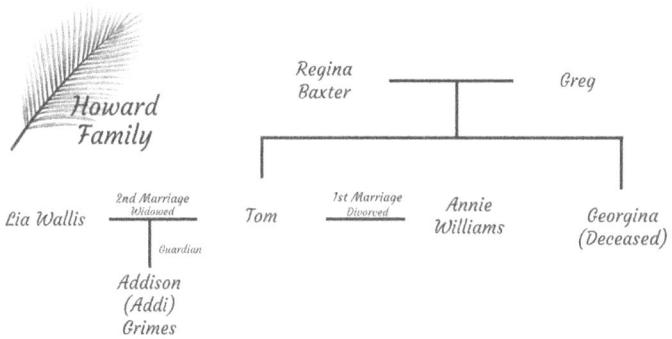

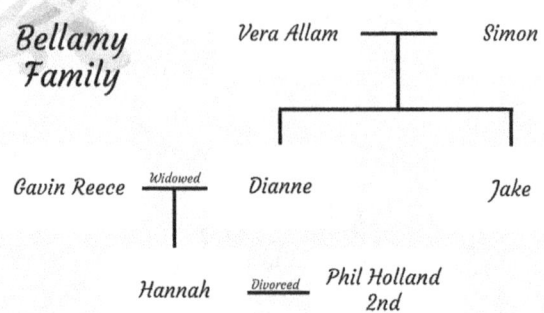

Bellamy Family

Vera Allam —— Simon
            |
   ┌────────┴────────┐
Gavin Reece —Widowed— Dianne   Jake
         |
      Hannah —Divorced— Phil Holland 2nd

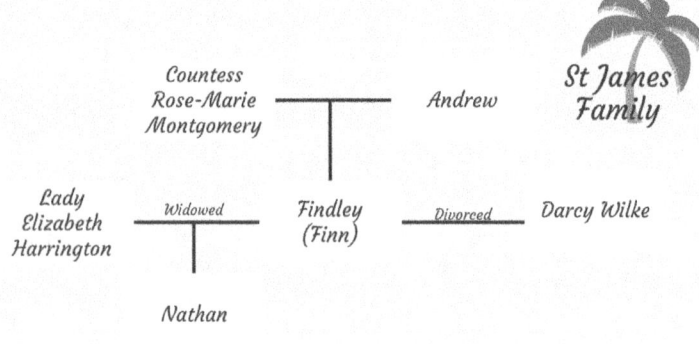

St James Family

Countess Rose-Marie Montgomery —— Andrew
                    |
Lady Elizabeth Harrington —Widowed— Findley (Finn) —Divorced— Darcy Wilke
                    |
                 Nathan

Chapter One
AN ANNIVERSARY OF TRUTH - PART ONE

THREE MONTHS AGO

*A*nnie had just finished setting the table under the gazebo at the end of their dock. It overlooked the lazy river where rays of silver from the full moon staring down at it glistened across its surface. She hadn't had time to cook, instead, she had ordered Roger's favorite meal from the Italian restaurant in the village. Annie checked the ice bucket to ensure the champagne was chilling as it should be. She gave the table a last once over, making sure it was perfect for hers and Roger's thirty-seventh wedding anniversary. It was the first time their children were unable to make it back home for their anniversary, so they'd decided to have a quiet romantic night at home.

Annie looked at her wristwatch. She still had forty-five minutes to shower and change before Roger got home. Annie had just walked through the glass patio doors that led into the back living room when the front door opened, and Roger walked in. The minute Annie saw his face, her heart dropped, and the welcoming smile on her lips faded away. Something was wrong. Her heart skipped a beat when her first thought was that something had happened to one of the children. Annie was about to ask him when he interrupted her.

"We need to talk, Annie," Roger's voice was flat, emotionless, and his eyes reflected its tone.

"Is everything alright?" Annie's heart was now beating so heavily in her chest she felt as if she was running a marathon.

"No, it's not, and it hasn't been for a very long time." Roger looked down at the floor, rubbing the back of his neck.

Annie's brow creased into a confused frown. "Has something happened at work?"

Roger and one of his college friends had started a filming and photography studio that filmed documentaries. They were hired by network studios to photograph and film breaking news from all around the world. A couple of years ago his friend had pulled out of the business and Roger had been forced to take on a silent partner. They had started branching out into short films, music videos, and documentaries. The new partnership had been good for Roger's company so much so a major film studio was looking to buy them out, but that deal would only happen in another ten months or so. By the sound of Roger's voice and the look on his face, Annie wondered if maybe the film studio was withdrawing its interest in the business.

"No, it's not about work," Roger said. "Work is ..." He cleared his throat. "I don't think I'm going to be selling by the end of the year Annie."

"Did the film company pull out of wanting to buy it?" Annie asked him, her frown deepening.

"I just don't think I'm ready to pack my career in for at least another two years," Roger told her.

"But I thought we were going to enjoy an early retirement together, so while we are still young enough to enjoy what we made of our lives and see the world together," Annie reminded him. "That's why I sold the art gallery this year."

"I'm still aiming to do that," Roger informed her before bluntly stating, "Only, I'm not going to be enjoying my retirement years with you, Annie."

"I don't understand." Annie felt tiny shock waves zing up her spine and stab at her brain. She wondered if she should pinch herself because she'd maybe dozed off and was having a bad dream.

"Look, Annie, there is no easy way to say this." Roger looked her straight in the eye. "But I want a divorce."

"What?" Annie asked him stupidly, wondering if she'd heard him correctly. Was he asking for a divorce on the day of their wedding anniversary?

Annie's eyes searched his looking for some sign that this was some sick joke he was playing for their anniversary or a belated April's fool prank.

"Our marriage isn't working anymore," Roger said. "It's time for me to move on."

"Move on?" Annie knew she sounded like a parrot repeating words.

She was trying to understand how Roger had left that morning with a smile on his face, kissed her goodbye, and went off to the office as he always did only to come home asking for a divorce? What had happened? Did he go to work and suddenly realize he no longer love her it was time to move on?

"Don't you love me anymore is that what you're trying to tell me?" Annie rubbed the base of her throat. "Did I do something wrong?"

"Oh, Annie, I will always love you," Roger assured her. "You've done nothing wrong. I can assure you this is all me."

"Then why are you wanting to break up our marriage?" Annie asked him. "If you still love me, how could you just suddenly want to walk away from our life?" She shook her head. "How did you go off this morning after wishing me happy anniversary only to come home wanting a divorce?" Annie asked him, her voice echoing her confusion. "If you were unhappy, why have you never said anything? Maybe we could try to fix what's making you unhappy or go to marriage counselling?"

Her frown deepened as a desperation to understand his sudden change of heart built up inside of her. Annie felt like

3

someone had thrown a brick through her happy life shattering it to pieces. Annie wasn't quite sure if the scene unfolding in front of her was real or some terrible dream. Flashes of another time in her life when she was blindsided by a marriage breakup hammered through her head.

How can this be happening? Annie's mind screamed.

"Annie, you can't change the way someone feels or fix everything that's wrong, no matter how hard you try," Roger's eyes darkened with emotion. "Trust me. I know that from thirty-seven years of experience. No counselling is going to help us."

Annie was stunned at his words. "Why now?" She asked him. "Why today, of all days?"

"Because I can't deny how I feel about Rochelle any longer," Roger told her dropping a bombshell on her that felt like it exploded in her chest.

"Rochelle?" Shock waves ricocheted through Annie's system. "Your assistant Rochelle?" Roger nodded in confirmation. "Isn't she younger than our youngest daughter?" She couldn't stop the drop of spite that weaved its way into her voice.

"No," Roger said, his brows creasing into an expressive frown. "Rochelle is thirty-eight."

"Oh, so she's a little older than Mark and Sage then," Annie had to fight to control the sharp barbs springing from her tongue. "That makes it so much better. Our children's new stepmother will be a few years older than them."

"I'm sorry, Annie." Roger's voice dropped. "But I couldn't go on any longer the way I was. I'm in love with her and I'm tired of feeling guilty about Rochelle."

"Feeling guilty..." Annie's eyes widened as she realized what Roger was admitting. "Please tell me this is something that's just happened and that you haven't been —"

Annie watched Roger's Adam's apple bob in his throat as he swallowed, closed his eyes, and took a deep breath before facing her again.

"I'm so sorry, Annie." Roger's voice was soft and hoarse with emotion. "But it just happened."

"It just happened?" Annie hissed. "You mean it just happened today? Yesterday? A week ago? When exactly, did this all *just* happen?"

"About two years ago," Roger held her gaze steadily, dropping his hands to his sides.

"Oh!" Annie flinched and felt like he'd actually struck her.

They stood in a tense silence for a few seconds that seemed to drag on making like minutes had passed by before Roger broke the silence.

"My lawyer told me to give you these so we can start the process as soon as possible." Roger pulled her back from her thoughts when he reached into his jacket pocket and pulled out a large, folded envelope. He handed it to her. "I've been advised to say no more about the divorce to you. Any discussions about money, assets, or the terms of the divorce should be handled through our lawyers."

"You've already gone to a lawyer?" Annie's eyes widened in surprise at how fast this was all moving. "I'm not leaving my house."

She didn't know why she said that, and Annie appalled at how angry and spiteful she'd sounded. Almost like she was angrier about the thought of losing her house than him.

Roger said nothing all he did was nodded. He ran his hand over his face before starting to turn to leave. "I'm going to grab some of my things I need. I will arrange to get the rest another time and may need to ask you if I could store some of my items with you?" He looked at her questioningly. "Just until I'm settled again."

"Sure," Annie agreed. "Go ahead." She gestured toward the stairs to their room with her hand. "I'll leave you to it."

Before Roger could say anything else, Annie turned and walked out of the patio doors and down to the dock. While Roger packed to leave their home and marriage, Annie cleared off the table she'd set to celebrate another year of their life together. A life she thought they were going to live together for the rest of their lives. Annie's mind reeled and she knew she had to keep busy at least until Roger had left. If she didn't Annie feared, she'd break down into an emotional heap. Then all the anger, outrage, and hurt would erupt from within her to drown Roger for his stinging betrayal.

Annie had just finished cleaning up and was standing at the patio doors staring out across the back garden to the river when Roger finally came back down. She turned to see that he'd packed two large suitcases.

"So, is this really happening?" Annie looked at him, her eyes searching his for a sign that this was some weird dream or crazy test.

He looked at her and nodded, "Are you okay, Annie?" Roger put his suitcases down at the door and walked over to her.

"I'm not too sure," Annie answered him honestly. "Can I get back to you about that when the shock wears off?"

Roger gave her a sad smile before shoving his hands in his jeans' pockets. He looked past her and toward the river as if gathering his thoughts.

"I am going to miss our home," Roger's gaze stayed fixed on the back garden.

"But not enough to stay," Annie felt the tight control she had on her emotions starting to slip, she cleared her throat.

"You know I will always love you and be here for you, Annie." Roger looked at her. "I'm just not in love with you anymore." He looked back out towards the river, shuffling awkwardly on his feet. "Our journey together has come to an end."

"I thought we were about to start a new journey together?" Annie felt her eyes fill with tears and swiped furiously at the stray drops that splashed down her cheeks. Her voice was soft and raspy, "You promised you'd never hurt me or leave me alone."

"Oh, Annie. You're not alone." Roger gently wiped another tear from her cheek. "This hasn't been easy for me." He shoved his hand back into the pocket of his jeans. "The last thing I ever wanted was to hurt you. But the longer I stay with you the more I'm hurting both of us."

"The way I see it," Annie sniffed. "I'm the only one here that's hurting."

"No, Annie, I've been hurting too." Roger shook his head denying her allegation. "I've loved you my whole life and I have done some crazy things for you. I would've turned the world upside down to have you look at me even just once the way you looked at ..." He glance out at the river again, shaking his head. "I thought that in time I would become your first love and you would fall as hopelessly in love with me as I was with you. But it never happened but I still had you in my life and it was an amazing life. You filled it with love, laughter, and joy." He let out a breath. "I thought it would be enough and for a long time I was content to settle for what we had but then the kids started to make their own way in life. That is when I realized it was the love we shared for them that was keeping us together."

"Are you blaming me for your infidelity?" Annie looked at him in amazement through a watery haze. "Are you accusing me of not loving you enough that you had to go out and find someone who could?"

"No, Annie, I know you love me," Roger told her, looking her in the eyes. "And I'm not blaming you for anything." He took in another deep breath. "But can I be honest with you?"

"I thought we always were honest with each other, Roger!" Annie's eyes narrowed. "At least I know I always have been with you."

"Really, Annie?" Roger's eyes flashed and he raised his eyebrows. "I may have cheated on you in the last couple of years and while you never cheated on me physically can your really say the same emotionally throughout our entire marriage?"

"What are you talking about?" Annie looked at him questioningly. "Is this still about my passion for ballet and you thinking it was my only true love?"

"If only it was just ballet that I've had to compete with all these years!" Roger said, frustratedly.

"Compete with?" Annie was growing more and more confused.

"I'm talking about *him!*" Roger grated and before Annie could say anything he continued. "Do you know that one of the best days of my life was when you said yes to being my girlfriend in high school. I was so in love with you I didn't care that I was your second love. I knew ballet would probably always be your first." He gave a small laugh. "But that didn't keep me from hoping that your passion for ballet would fade. That it would one day be me that put such passion in your heart that it lit up your soul making you shine like the beautiful light you are."

"Roger..." Annie's eyes widened in surprise at his words and tears started to well up in her eyes once again. "I did... do love you!"

"Annie, I know you love me, and you poured everything into our marriage, our family, our home. I couldn't have asked for a better mother for my children or partner over these past thirty-seven years," Roger assured her. "But I realized many years ago that I only had the tiniest piece of your heart," he admitted. "The part that I wanted didn't belong to me and never will."

"Roger, I..." Annie felt her throat constrict at the pain she saw in his eyes.

"None of this is your fault, Annie. There is no blame here because you can't help who you fall in love with." Roger put his hands on the top of her arms, leaned in and kissed her forehead. "I never should've cheated on you, Annie. It was wrong of me and I'm so sorry. I hope one day you can forgive me for my indiscretions and the stupid things I've done." He stepped back and dropped his hands from her arms. "You didn't deserve that from me. You don't know how many times I wanted to come clean and tell you."

The mention of Roger's infidelity hit her like an arrow through her heart once again bringing back the hurt, anger, and pain from his betrayal. Annie felt like her mind and emotions were reaching overload. She needed to be alone to process before she said something she would regret. Her mother always told her that if her heart was filled with hurt, anger, or bitterness it was better to keep her tongue still in order to avoid later regret.

"It's getting late and if you don't mind, I'd like to be alone," Annie glanced at the door where his luggage was. "I'll make an appointment with my lawyer first thing in the morning."

Roger stared at her for a few seconds before nodding and walking back to the front door.

"Goodbye, Annie," Roger said, opening the front door before bending to pick up his cases. "Take care of yourself."

Chapter Two
AN ANNIVERSARY OF TRUTH - PART TWO

PRESENT DAY

Annie looked at the three legal documents lying on the kitchen counter in front of her. Two of them were like well-aimed arrows to her heart, shattering a lifetime of happy memories. The third one was supposed to mark the start of her and her husband's, Roger's, next phase of their life, the beginning of their early retirement. She picked the third document up and looked at it. The final papers for the sale of her New York City art Gallery. Her business she'd lovingly grown for thirty-four years.

Roger was supposed to be selling his business at the end of the year to join her in an early retirement. Until then, she had been looking forward to taking time to concentrate on her garden, and finally getting to do some painting. She was even looking forward to trying out all the recipes she'd clipped over the years and never got around to making. She had plans to take some me time and enjoy all the things she'd always been too busy to enjoy. She was even toying with the idea of accepting the local ballet schools offer for her to teach ballet. But none of that mattered now because all her plans had been broken. She put the deed of transfer back onto the counter top.

She leaned her hands on the shiny soft pink marble surface and closed her eyes. She remembered how she had been in two minds when it came time to finally put her gallery on the market. It had felt like she was selling one of her children or saying goodbye to another of her career dreams. Annie had built that gallery from the ground up to what it was today. She hadn't even had to list the business to sell it. That was how renowned and successful, she had made it. Before and during the sale, she had gone through a myriad of up and down emotions about selling her precious art gallery. It had probably been her subconscious warning her something wasn't right in what she thought was her happy life.

Annie looked at the document in the middle of the other two. A few pink tabs were sticking out on one side, marking the pages that needed to be signed. Her heart felt heavy looking down at it. While the one on the left marked the end of her business and career, this one marked the end of a thirty-seven-year marriage. The splitting of her life with Roger and everything they'd built together.

She lifted her head to look out the window of her old colonial-style house standing in a sought-after neighborhood on the banks of the Connecticut River in Greenwich – the home her four children had grown up in. Her eyes turned to the wall next to the breakfast table. Her children's height charts still marked the wall showing their growing progress from the first year they moved in. They would measure their growth progress on the morning of their birthdays. Annie's and Roger's heights were also on the wall. The kids would see how fast they were catching up to their parents each year. Up until the kids were about eleven it had been a fun competition to see who had grown the most.

Her son, Mark, the second eldest by and hour, had shot up at seventeen to where he was today at six-foot-four. Her eldest daughter, Sage, Mark's twin sister, was five-foot-eight. Craig,

Annie's third, was six-foot-two while the baby of the family, Emily, was the shorty at five-foot-five, just like Annie. She smiled, remembering each birthday they had held here, the anniversaries, their Christmases, and all the special moments. All shared between the walls of what she always thought of as a happy home full of love. She closed her eyes once again and swallowed down the burning lump forming in her throat.

Annie looked down at the third document. That was the hardest one, and she knew she'd have to decide soon. It was an offer on the house. She had gone through it a few times, looking for something she could use to turn it down or nitpick about to draw the matter out. But there was nothing the contract was sound. The buyer had also placed an offer over her asking price of the house. The sale also didn't depend on when he sold his current property. It meant that the sale would go through without a hitch or delay. She glanced around the room she was standing in. It wasn't just a room for her or a house. It was the home she and Roger had spent so many happy years watching their children grow up. Each room was like an album of memories with a story.

She walked out of the kitchen and into the back living room that opened up to the back patio. It overlooked the lazy river that meandered past their garden. In the tall oak tree to the one side was the tree-house Roger and Sage had built a few months after they moved in. She smiled, remembering eleven-year-old Sage planning just how she wanted the tree house to look. Sage had even researched what wood was the strongest as one day Sage wanted hers and her siblings' kids to play in it, so it had to last. She had bombarded the local hardware owner with so many questions he'd become Annie's and Roger's first friend in Greenwich. Pete Saunders was still a good friend of theirs, and it was through him that they'd found a buyer for the house so quickly.

Her eyes moved to the swings and jungle gym that stood not too far from the tree. She could still see Sage and her twin brother, Mark, pushing their two younger siblings on the swings and helping them on the jungle gym. Sage and Mark were only two when Craig had been born, but Sage had instantly taken on the role of protective big sister, and it was the same when Emily was born two years after Craig. While Mark was the broodier intellect type that preferred to outwit rather than outgun or threaten, Sage wasn't scared to get her hands dirty. She shook her head remembering all the times Sage's big heart and overprotective nature had gotten her into trouble or spats. Her eldest daughter couldn't stand seeing injustice.

Sage was still like that. Except now, she was using those skills to save the world one truth-hitting article, or news report at a time. Thinking of Sage working made her think how quickly time had flown. One minute her children were babies, and the next, they had become teenagers too soon they had left home. Now Sage and Mark were thirty-six, Craig was thirty-four, and Emily was thirty-two. Just when she was ready to start hinting that it was time for grandbabies, her life had been turned upside down. She'd sold her livelihood, signed away her marriage, and was about to sell her family's home.

She looked up, surprised to find herself standing on the small dock that jutted out into the river. It was hers and Roger's favorite place to sit and unwind on a clear evening during summer or winter. They'd sit on their chairs with a glass of wine and chat while they enjoyed each other's company and watched the moon cast silver shadows over the rippling water. She loved to come and stand out here in the early morning with her cup of coffee before everyone in the house woke up for a few moments of peace before the hustle and bustle began. She slowly turned around and looked back at their six-bedroom two-story colonial house that she'd fallen in love with the minute she'd seen it. She had known the second she walked through the gate this was going to be their home.

How did one just pack up a house full of memories? Would the new owner miss the wall with her children's height chart or the tall oak tree with the tree house? How do you pack those things to take with you? While she could move all their tangible memories like photos and childhood keepsakes, how did she move the ones that were now part of the house? Annie was drawn from her thoughts when she heard the voice of her youngest, Emily, calling her. She frowned and started walking back into the house.

What is Emily doing at home? she wondered, hoping everything was alright with her daughter because she wasn't due home for another week.

"Em?" Annie called. "I'm out in the back, honey."

"Oh, hey, mom." Emily met her halfway to the house, giving Annie a hug and kiss on the cheek. "Sorry to just drop in, but I have a few days off after doing my fair share of filling in for our understaffed airline."

"Hello, my baby," Annie greeted Emily. "You work so hard. But honey, why are you not spending these few days off with your fiancé?"

"Because..." Emily didn't get to finish her sentence when Sage walked through the door.

"She and Nate have been broken up for some months now," Sage butted in and finished Emily's sentence for her. "Hi, mom." She squeezed in between Annie and Emily to hug her.

"Sage!" Emily hissed at her older sister. "Why do you always have to do that?"

"Because I knew you'd chicken out telling mom," Sage told her. "You'd then shy away from telling the truth for a few days before breaking down and eventually telling mom about it. So, I saved you a lot of stressing over it."

"She's right, Em," Mark's voice had Annie looking past her two girls to see her son walking towards them. "You do that all the time."

"Hi, mommy!" Mark pushed past his sisters, pulled Annie into a big hug, and planted a kiss on her head as he towered over his mother. Mark kept his one arm around Annie's shoulders while she wrapped her arm around his waist. "How are you holding up, mom?"

"Truthfully, I think having to sell the house is the hardest part for me," Annie told them. "Before we discuss my woes – not that I'm complaining because it's such a lovely surprise – what are you all doing here?"

"We knew this would be hard for you," Craig's voice came from behind her, making her jump and spin around. Letting go of Mark's waist to open her opens out to him. Craig scooped Annie up as he always did, twirled her, and kissed her cheek before putting her down. "So, we all decided to surprise you and help you make the decision."

Also, Sage got fired. She had a failed summer romance and gave notice on her loft in Soho," Emily told Annie, then gave her sister a smug smile. "See, I can also make things much simpler by blurting it all out to mom right away."

"I never got fired!" Sage glared at Emily. "I quit my job. Summer romances never last, and my lease was about to expire, so I decided not to renew it."

"Oh, honey," Annie said, leaving Craig's side to pull her daughter into an embrace. "It's going to be okay." She pulled away from Sage and looked at all four of her beautiful children. "We're all going to be okay."

For the first time since Roger's divorce bombshell, Annie actually believed it.

"Do you have anything to eat?" Craig asked. "I've had a very long journey, and I'm starving."

"Of course," Annie said. "Let's go inside, and I'll make us a snack."

The five of them started to walk back to the house.

Annie saw all her children's luggage piled up near the stairs as they walked through to the front of the house. The house once again felt warm and full.

"Oh, while we're tattling on our siblings, Mark has decided to do yet another marine something or other degree before downgrading and taking a position at a small marine center." Craig grinned at his older brother's black glare.

"Is that true?" Annie looked up at her eldest son.

"Yes, I'm going back to university in a few weeks' time," Mark told her. "The new position does not pay as much as I've been earning, but the perks are a lot better, and so are the hours. I also get to work with marine life, and the center is funding my next degree." Mark smiled down at Annie. "I'm actually looking forward to it."

"As long as you're happy, my baby," Annie told him. "That's all I could ask for, for all of you."

They walked inside, and Annie went to put the kettle on while her children took their bags up to their rooms to get settled in. She stopped for a few seconds before starting to make some food and listened to the commotion her children brought with them, smiling. Her heart felt better about letting go of the house. After all, home was where her family was. Wherever she ended up after this, she knew her children would support and follow her. They would set down new roots and make even more happy memories wherever they were.

She may not be that lucky with relationships, but she'd hit the jackpot with her children. They were her heart and soul, as well as the only relationship that really mattered in the end.

Chapter Three
LETTING GO OF YESTERDAY

Later that evening, Annie and her kids were sitting in the back living room with steaming mugs of cocoa. As it was the middle of spring, the evenings could still get cold. They were going through old photo albums. Laughing about good childhood memories, arguing about the times they got into trouble and whose fault it had been, as well as feeling moments of sadness with the ones that hurt. Annie loved evenings like this with her children, and while she'd like their family to stay the size it was, she did look forward to when her children found their soul mates.

Her eyes fell on Emily. Annie knew her baby was hurting inside, but like Emily always did, she bottled it all up. Annie wished she could take her baby in her arms and tell her it would be okay. But she had to wait for Emily to come to her when she was ready to deal with whatever happened between her and Nate. Annie liked Nate. He was an airline pilot, which is how he and Emily had met. He also had impeccable manners and Annie had thought he was madly in love with Emily, and she wondered what had happened between the two of them.

Emily and Nate had been dating for a year before they got engaged two years ago. Annie had stopped asking Emily when they would set a date after the first year of the engagement. All Emily would ever say was that they were too busy, and when the airline was back on track with regular flights as well as more staff, they would talk about it. In other words, Emily and Nate were not ready to get married and were enjoying their engaged commitment to each other. They were both adventurers that loved to explore and try new things. Emily's motto was to try something new whenever you got the opportunity – even if it scared you to death. No one gets out of life alive, so you may as well live each day and look for adventure in every moment. Because if you had a big enough imagination climbing a flight of stairs could be getting you ready for your first mountain climb. Even though Emily was laughing and looking like she was participating in the evening of fun her smile never reached her eyes. Her baby girl was hurting inside, and all Annie wanted to do was somehow take that hurt away.

"Oh, wow, mom." Emily's voice cut through Annie's thoughts. "Look, this is you with us the year before grandma died."

Annie leaned forward and took the photo from Emily. Her heart lurched when she saw the picture. Roger had taken it at the Manatee Sanctuary that her parents owned, in Manatee Bay, Florida. Annie was standing between her mother and father with her four children standing in front of the four adults. Sage and Mark were nine, Craig was seven, and Emily was five. Annie's heart twinged at the memory of the last holiday in Manatee Bay. It was the last time Annie had seen her mother as she knew her. Once cancer took hold of her for the second time, her mother had declined rapidly, and the last time she'd seen her was in the hospital.

"We never went back to Manatee Bay after grandma passed away," Mark pointed out.

"The year after grandmother passed was a very busy time both work and family-wise for your father and me," Annie explained. "It always made more sense for granddad to come here for the holidays. Especially after we bought this house."

"Would you go back there now that you and dad are getting divorced, and you've sold the gallery?" Sage asked Annie, taking the photo from her to look at it. "I love spending time in the sanctuary with granddad."

"You mean you loved bossing everyone around at the sanctuary," Mark reminded her.

"I never bossed anyone around. There were just a few things they could've done better," Sage defended her actions.

"Sage, you don't even know you're bossing people around under the guise of looking out for them." Craig laughed and put his arm around her shoulders, giving her a squeeze. "We all love you for caring enough about us to boss us around."

He gave her a cheeky grin, and Sage punched him on the arm, "You're still such a brat."

"You know I was only playing," Craig smiled at his older sister. "No, but really, sis, you always put us first throughout your entire life, making sure we were all okay."

"You made sure no one bullied us or hurt us in any way," Emily added to the list of what Sage was to them. "You were always the one that was tough and pushed back, so we didn't have to be."

"Although you did teach us how to be tough when we needed to be," Craig told her. "You were an extension of our beautiful, loving mother."

"Hey, I looked out for you both as well," Mark said, feigning hurt feelings.

"Of course, you did, big brother," Craig slapped Mark on the back. "You and Sage had your good cop bad cop routine down so well that every kid for miles around us was scared of the two of you."

"They called you the night and day twins," Emily reminded them.

"That was because of our contrasting hair color," Mark pointed out. "Mine is dark, and Sage's is blond."

"No, it was because even though Sage was tough, she was always sunny," Craig told him.

"While you, Mark, were the dark, broody guy that everyone thought quite mysterious," Emily finished for Craig. "For twins, you and Sage are polar opposites."

"Not in everything," Sage said. "For instance, we both..." She looked at Mark for help.

"Don't like pineapple," was the only thing Mark could come up with. "Or motorbikes."

"Wow!" Craig laughed. "Is that all the two of you could come up with?"

"Okay, so we're not much alike." Sage laughed too. "Oh, we're both bossy, organized, love to research, and win in the boardgame Thirty Seconds every time."

"You two only win all the time because you play as a team, and while you may not be a lot alike, you still have that twin bond, telepathy thing advantage on us," Emily accused.

"We always offered to play with one of you, but you two were always determined to beat us," Sage reminded them. "Besides, we only have one because mom and dad let us. If they didn't fake not knowing the answers, they would've won family game night every Saturday night."

"Why do you think your father and I would let you win?" Annie hid her smile.

Annie and Roger loved family game night. Watching their kids interact, laugh, argue, and get up to crazy antics, always made them feel so lucky to have had such great kids. The four of them were close and called each other nearly every day. Annie had been an only child. Her childhood best friend back in Manatee Bay, Dianne Bellamy, had a baby brother, Jake, and even though he was ten years younger than them, he and Dianne were close. When Jake didn't have his nose in a book or was trying to save something or someone, he'd be with them as Dianne took care of him while her mother worked. Annie didn't have a sibling to bicker with, look after, or watch television with. When her parents were working or out on date night, it was just Annie and her babysitter. That is why Annie had wanted three or four children of her own so they would have each other.

"So, mom..." Mark leaned forward and put his empty mug on the coffee table. "Are we going to have a family meeting to discuss the issues of these past three months?"

"Mark!" Sage hissed at her brother and shook her head. "Why do you always have to be so stiff and talk around a subject?"

"What our stuffy intellect brother was trying to say is," Craig took over the conversation before Mark and Sage started to argue. "Can we finally talk about the house and dad?"

Annie knew she'd have to talk to them sooner or later, but she was hoping for later. They were an open and honest family. When one of them was having a problem, they all were because they'd come together to help each other out, support, or be a shoulder to cry on. Even though her children were adults, the divorce, and sale of their family home affected them as well. When Annie was considering selling the gallery, she'd first discussed it with her children. After all, if she'd kept the gallery, one day it would've been the legacy she'd left for them. But her children just wanted her to be happy, and even though they'd loved her gallery, it had been her passion, so they'd supported her selling it. And after the shock she'd recently received about Roger's business, Annie was now glad that she had sold it when she did.

Annie looked at the four faces staring expectantly back at her waiting for her to respond. She also knew they were still angry at their father for cheating on Annie and devastated about the divorce. She'd felt so sorry for poor Roger when they'd got the children together to tell them they were divorcing. They had met in New York at in their New York apartment. It had been one of the most uncomfortable family gatherings ever. Annie had hardly said a word and let Roger tell them the news, only speaking when she was required to answer. The children had been stunned into silence when he dropped the bombshell about the divorce. Before anyone could ask if Roger and Annie had tried to work things out, Annie had blurted out that Roger no longer loved her and that he was seeing someone else.

That was when the devastation of the divorce turned into anger. As the penny dropped, her children realized that their father had been having an affair. Roger hadn't tried to deny it. Instead, he was open and honest with his children about it and bore the brunt of their anger. Roger let them all have their say and told them he would always love their mother, but he was no longer in love with her, and that was not her fault or the children's. None of this was anyone's fault but his, and he'd not been happy for years before he met Rochelle. Roger explained that he and Annie had gotten married when they were only eighteen after being childhood sweethearts. He told them he wasn't leaving any of them. He was still their father, and Annie would always be his first big love. But they were now on different paths and wanted other things in life. When he met Rochelle, he didn't mean to fall in love with her, and Roger never wanted to hurt his family.

But the children weren't ready to hear him out or listen to his story. All they saw were excuses from a man who'd cheated on their mother. For two years, Roger had kept his affair secret instead of coming clean right from the start. None of them begrudged him or their mother for being happy, but Annie and Roger had brought them up with good moral compasses. Their children were brought up with parents who told them that while the truth could hurt or get them into trouble, it was better to be upfront. Skirting around the truth, keeping it, or telling a lie, only makes it escalate into something they may not be able to come back from. Yet Roger had not only lied to them for two years, but he lived that lie.

After two hours, Roger had to go. Before he went, he told the children that when they were ready, he'd really like them to meet Rochelle because they were getting engaged as soon as the divorce came through. Roger really should not have told them that. It was too soon after all the bombshells he'd just dropped on them. As far as Annie knew, neither Mark, Sage, Craig, or Emily had spoken to Roger since that day. Craig actually had not spoken to his father even before the news of the divorce. When

Annie had asked if he and his father had a falling out, Craig had denied it. He put it down to just not having the time and heavy schedules. But Annie knew something had happened between the two of them because Craig and his father had always been close up until whatever happened between them.

Chapter Four
MOVING ON - PART ONE

Annie bit her lip, wondering if there was any way she could once again wiggle out of talking about the divorce and selling the house. Because she knew if they started to ask questions, Annie would be forced to tell her children the truth, which would only make them even angrier with their father. Especially now that Annie had made the mistake of telling Sage, she didn't know where she would go once the house sold. She wasn't sure what she could afford to buy from what she'd end up with after the sale. Annie had said that without thinking, as her mind had been in quite a turmoil when she'd found out she'd have to sell the house. When Sage had asked her what she'd meant by that, Annie had fobbed it off and changed the subject quickly. But she knew her daughter would not have forgotten about the conversation, and she would've told her siblings.

"Mom?" Emily smiled at her. "You know you will have to speak to us sometime about this, right?"

"Yes, especially when you have two journalists in the family that, if they haven't already done so, will go digging up everything they need to know," Mark warned her. "I don't need to tell you that they will leave no stone unturned, and I'm sure even our angelic mother has some secrets hidden beneath one."

Annie's eyes flew to her eldest son in shock. Surely, he couldn't possibly know...

"Relax, mom," Sage patted her mother's hand. "Mark is only pulling your strings."

"It's okay, honey," Annie sighed, resignedly but was still feeling slightly uncomfortable with what Mark had just said. Because some secrets were better left under their rock in the past.

"All kidding aside, though, mom," Mark leaned back and crossed his ankle over his knee. "We were all surprised when you said you had to sell the house."

"Why would you sell it, mom?" Emily looked at Annie expectantly. "The house is paid for, and as far as we know, you paid off two-thirds of that. As the divorce was instigated by dad and he cheated on you, surely your lawyer can get him to relinquish his third of it?"

"Yes, why do you have to leave your home because he walked out?" Craig's voice was full of anger and disgust. "Dad has a successful business. Plus, won't you have to split up the pension fund that the two of you have been saving up since you started working?"

"Yes, and that would be split equally because you and dad put in the same amount each month," Sage pointed out. "You've always told us that you and dad had more than enough to live comfortably and do everything you ever wanted while still leaving a tidy sum for us to inherit one day."

"As you and dad are splitting all the shared assets and then keeping the ones you each asked for, surely you could've asked for the house?" Emily repeated what she had said before. "This is your home, and like I said before, you shouldn't have to be forced to uproot your life because he wanted out of our family."

"Honey, you know he's still your father. I'm the one he's divorcing, and not you," Annie told her.

"As far as we're all concerned, he divorced us too," Sage backed up her younger sister. "He taught us to be honest, loyal, and true to ourselves and the ones we love."

"Look, I know you're still all angry and disillusioned by your father," Annie looked at each of them. "But I know it was never his intention to hurt any of you. He has always been a great dad who was there for each of you."

"Yes, but now that we're grown up, he..." Craig's eyes narrowed. "He doesn't think we need him anymore, so he went looking for someone else who did." He shook his head and Annie could see how angry Craig was at him. "Mom..." He stopped and shook his head. "I'm sorry."

"Thank you, sweetheart." Annie gave him a small smile.

"I agree with Craig," Emily said. "He didn't give one hoot that you needed him, especially now that you'd sold the gallery at his urging if I may add. You're the one that is alone now, and on top of that, he's making you sell the house?"

"Mom, why don't you just buy dad's one third of the house from him with some of your half of the pension fund?" Mark suggested. "That way, we get to keep our home."

"If only it were that simple, my love." Annie sighed, knowing she'd have to tell them the truth. "I did think about buying out the portion of the house that your father owned."

Annie knew this was only going to be another mark against Roger. But the children were going to find out one way or the other, and it was better if it came from her.

"And?" Sage's eyes narrowed as she stared at Annie. "Was he not happy with what you were offering him?"

"It wasn't that, honey," Annie told her. "There is no easy way to say this."

"Then just tell us what is going on," Emily said impatiently.

"When your father and I met with our attorneys to go over the splitting of assets and closing of joint accounts." Annie swallowed and shook her head.

"Mom, what is it you're having such a hard time telling us?" Sage asked.

Annie breathed out, bit her lip, and said, "When I suggested that I keep the house, your father's lawyer said that was not going to be an option." Annie shook her head.

"Because your father needed the money from share of the sale."

"Dad needed the money?" Mark's brow creased into a frown. "Why on earth would he need the money when his company is doing so well? And didn't you say you would let him keep the New York apartment?" He shook his head. "Which, I must say, I thought a little odd considering your grandfather had left it to you to keep in your family."

"No, who said I was going to give him the New York apartment?" Annie looked at Mark, shocked and confused. "Who told you that?"

"His girlfriend told me a few weeks ago," Mark's frown deepened. "She's moved in with him there."

"I'm sorry," Annie stopped the conversation and looked at Mark in amazement. "Did you just say that Rochelle was living in our New York apartment with your father?"

"You didn't know?" Sage looked at her mother in shock. "Dad told Mark that you knew."

"When did you talk to dad?" Emily asked Mark before anyone else could.

"It wasn't planned," Mark assured Emily. "I was in New York a couple of weeks ago for a meeting. It ran late, and I couldn't get back to Boston. I know mom told us that dad was staying there until he found a new place. It is a large apartment, and I figured one night under the same roof as dad wouldn't be that bad."

"And when you went there, you found that Rochelle had moved in as well?" Annie was astounded.

"Yes, I'm sorry, mom, I really thought you knew," Mark told her.

"That apartment was left to me by my grandfather," Annie explained to him. "It was left solely to me and is not even part of the divorce settlement."

"I'm so glad you thought about doing a prenup, even if you did it two years or so after you got married," Emily said.

"My grandparents wanted the apartment to remain in my

family because it was the first place my grandparents ever owned," Annie told them. "They lived there for the first part of their life until they went to take over the Manatee Bay Inn and Sanctuary from my grandparents."

"Why would dad think you were giving it to him then?" Sage asked.

"I'm not sure, but it is something I need to find out, especially when it no longer belongs to me," Annie surprised them by saying. "It belongs to the four of you now."

"Seriously?" Craig asked, looking at her wide-eyed.

"Yes, when I sold the gallery and re-did my will, I asked my lawyer if he could help me transfer the ownership of the apartment into my four children's names." Annie felt the heat of anger starting to burn in her stomach once the initial shock of the news wore off. "Your father is only living in the apartment until he finds his own place to live."

"Which we hope will be soon as I know I could use an apartment to stay in right now," Sage said.

"I could, too," Emily admitted. "I'm moving out of mine and Nates apartment."

"I will talk to my lawyer in the morning and clear this up," Annie promised. "In the meantime, it is getting really late, and I think we should get to bed."

"Not until you tell us why you have to sell the house rather than want to sell it." Sage wasn't letting off the hook that easily.

"Fine, I can't buy out your father's one-third of the house," Annie looked out the window. "Because there is nothing for me to buy him out with."

"WHAT?" Mark, Sage, Emily, and Craig said all at once, staring at her in shock.

"Our pension fund, emergency fund, and even life insurance policies have all been cleaned out." Anger started to bubble up inside Annie once again at the mention of it.

"How?" Sage asked

"By whom?" Mark's eyes once again burned with anger. "Dad?"

"Yes, by your father," Annie admitted to them.

Her eyes caught a weird look on Craig's face other than the anger flickering in his eyes. It was almost as if Craig had somehow known what his father had done. *Is that why Craig hasn't spoken to his father for so long? Because he knew about the money? Or maybe Craig knew about Roger's affair?* The thoughts sprinted across Annie's mind.

"Why on earth would dad need all that money?" Emily looked at Annie, astounded.

"It seems your father's business had not been doing that well for a while," Annie told the four of them. "He had won a contract with some big movie production company. To fulfill the project, they had to invest in some heavy equipment, new premises, and staff."

"He over extended his reach," Mark filled in for Annie.

"I believe so. A few weeks into the project, the production company canceled the series." Annie took a deep breath. "Your father found his business in big trouble. He basically had nothing but debt and useless equipment. The worst thing about losing that contract was that your father had dropped a few of his regular, smaller well-paying clients. That project was supposed to go on for ten to fifteen years. It also paid more than all the smaller ones combined."

"So, he cleared out your nest egg and your security to save his company?" Craig hissed in disgust.

"He did it because another company offered to buy his, but they wouldn't take on his debt," Annie explained. "Your father did have every intention of paying it all back when the business sold."

"I bet that sale fell through," Emily guessed. "Now dad has nothing but a business he has to rebuild. That is why he needs the money from the house."

"Yes," Annie nodded. "Luckily, when I sold the gallery, I immediately split it into all of your trusts and invested the portion I kept for myself."

"So, he couldn't get any of that money!" Craig said, relieved.

"Mom, if you need that money back, please take my portion. You have given us more than enough over the years."

"Yes, mom, take mine back too," Emily offered, followed by Sage and then Mark.

"That is so sweet of all of you." Annie's eyes misted over at their gestures. "I will be fine with the proceeds I get from the house and when my other new investment starts to pay out."

"But until then?" Mark asked her worriedly. "Are you going to be okay?"

"Yes, sweetheart," Annie assured him. "I'm sure I'm going to be fine."

Annie hoped her smile would cover the overwhelming doubt that had been eating at her these past three months.

"But where are you going to go when you sell our house, mom?" Emily took Annie's hand comfortingly. "You can always kick dad and that woman out of our flat in New York."

"Your father also needs to get back on his feet." Annie had to fight down the anger upon hearing that Rochelle was living in their New York apartment.

"I have an idea." Emily spoke up after they had all fallen into silence.

Annie looked at Emily curiously. She was looking at the photo of them on holiday in Manatee Bay before looking up at Annie and then glancing over at Mark. That was when Annie realized her children had already planned something.

"Mom," Mark took over from his sister. "That new job I told you about..." He caught Annie's eye. "I am now the new director of the Manatee Bay Manatee Sanctuary."

Annie's eyes widened, and she stared at Mark in shock.

"Granddad didn't want to say anything to you because he knew what you were going through last summer. You had the sale of the gallery and remodeling the kitchen, then grandad broke his arm. You were so snowed under with everything." Sage took over from Mark. "But he dislocated his shoulder again last summer and had to have an operation on it."

"He what?" Annie's eyes widened even more, and her heart

started to hammer in her chest. Her father had torn his rotator cuff when he was a pro hockey player, and he'd had endless problems and operations on it over the years.

"He's fine, mom," Craig reassured her. "Since last summer, the four of us have been taking turns visiting Manatee Bay to help him."

"I also spent two days with grandad when I had a stopover in Key West a few days ago," Emily told her. "He has recovered nicely and is back at work."

"I can't believe I was so absorbed with everything that I didn't even know my father was in the hospital!" Annie said in dismay.

"Mom, trust us, we were all there for granddad," Sage promised her. "There was nothing you could've done anyway, and if it was life-threatening, we'd have let you know."

"Thank you, my darling children," Annie looked at them proudly. Her heart swelled to a bursting point with pride. "I always wonder how I got so lucky to have the best children in the world."

"Granddad has recovered nicely, mom, just like Emily said," Sage told her. "He's back trying to get the inn to open again. That is why he asked Mark to take over the sanctuary from him."

"I thought granddad wasn't reopening the inn this summer because the renovations were not nearly done?" Annie's brow creased into a confused frown.

"He's had some help from a few of the locals and is hopeful that he can fix up enough of the inn and a few rooms to open this summer. He has quite a few bookings," Emily explained. "That last storm that ripped through the island really damaged a big part of the inn. It was right after the storm that granddad hurt his arm and left it until he could barely use it before getting it seen to. That is the reason he had to have an operation on it."

"That sounds like something my father would do." Annie shook her head.

"Getting back to the idea of going to Manatee Bay," Sage

drew the conversation back to her. Annie frowned as Sage didn't sound as enthusiastic to go to Manatee Bay as her siblings did. "As Craig and I are between jobs and Emily has loads of holiday owing to her from the airline we thought we could all go there for the summer to help grandpops."

"I won't be able to join you though as I'm starting at the University of Florida on a summer course." Mark looked at his mother apologetically.

"Yes, our big brother has a new lady love in his life, and they are taking the course together," Craig looked teasingly at his brother who gave him a black look which as usual didn't faze Craig.

"New lady love?" Annie looked at Mark. "You didn't tell me you were seeing anyone again."

"I met her in Manatee Bay last summer. She works with her mother at the Manatee Sanctuary," Mark told Annie. "She and I have the same interests. We were both interested in this summer course and signed up for it together. It is still early, though and we don't want to rush into things. She's recently got a divorce and as you know I've been treading lightly with relationships since my last one."

"And who is this mystery woman?" Annie asked Mark.

"You know her mother!" Sage piped up before Mark had a chance to answer Annie.

"Oh?" Annie frowned.

"Yes, her unmarried name is Hannah Reece." Emily grinned and ducked the throw cushion Mark threw at her head.

"Hannah Reece?" Annie's eyes widened. "As in my life long best friend Dianne Reece's daughter?"

Chapter Five
MOVING ON - PART TWO

"Yes," Mark confirmed the name of the woman he was seeing. "I hope that is not going to be a problem for you, mom?" He looked at Annie, concerned by her shocked reaction.

"Oh, honey, no!" Annie realized what her expression must look like and softened it into a warm smile. "I couldn't be more delighted. You and Hannah are the perfect pair."

"They really are!" Craig said. "The good news is, Sage finally has competition in that board game, Thirty Seconds, because now Mark has a new partner."

Craig laughed at Sage's black look and defended her board game loss. "I was not in the best place when we played that game last summer."

"I think it will do us all the world of good to spend the summer in Manatee Bay at your family home, mom," Craig's eyes sparkled excitedly. "Besides, Grandpops needs all the help he can get with the inn's renovations." He puffed his chest up. "As you all know, I'm a darn good carpenter as my woodshop and projects around this house will attest to."

Emily got in on the action. "I can help for the summer and honestly I need to get away for a while." She gave a big sigh. "I'm looking forward to basking in the Florida sunshine."

"Granddad needs all the help he can get, especially as Florida is heading into its storm season soon," Craig told Annie. "We have to make sure the inn is as protected as we can get it, so all Grandpops new renovations aren't destroyed."

"Well, that's the four of us committed for the summer," Emily said.

Four pairs of eyes looked at Annie hopefully. She wasn't sure. Every time she'd gone back to spend a holiday with her parents after Sage and Mark were born it had been stressful. Annie had been on constant alert and kept looking over her shoulder in case she ran into the one person in the world she never wanted to see again. She knew that person had left Manatee Bay and rarely returned there. But there was always the chance. After her mother died, life got busier, and Annie had her own home to establish with a growing family, so getting back to Manatee Bay got harder each year. Which she was secretly glad about. There were just too many ghosts to haunt her back home.

Roger had never questioned her reluctance to go home after her mother passed away, and neither had her father. They had both thought it was because she couldn't bear to be there without her mother. She'd started to believe the excuse herself, right up until this moment with her children putting her on the spot. Annie knew she'd been painted into a corner. Her father needed help and had an operation she'd not even known about because he was concerned about what she was going through at the time. Annie had no option but to go, no matter how loud the voice in her heart was trying to warn her what a bad decision it was.

"I guess we're spending the summer in Manatee Bay." Annie managed to put on a brave smile, turning off all the warning bells ringing from her heart and soul.

"Grandpops will be so happy to have us all there." Emily clapped her hands together excitedly. "Do you mind if I tell him?" She pulled out her phone.

"Honey, why don't we call him together in the morning," Annie suggested looking at her wristwatch. "It's already ten."

"Okay." Emily sighed disappointedly. "I guess he can wait for the answer until then." She gave Annie a sweet smile as the penny dropped.

"Your grandfather already knows about this plan?" Annie looked at Emily accusingly and then at each of her other four children. "Were you all in on this?"

"Not me." Sage held up her hands defensively. "I was quite content to take you and me on some tropical island get-away for the summer."

"Not this again!" Emily shook her head at Sage. "You can go on a tropical island vacation next summer."

"And don't go blaming grandpops either," Mark said quickly, changing the subject back to Manatee Bay. "We were the ones that suggested this to him when we found out you were selling the house."

"Did you four already know about the money?" Annie's eyes narrowed as she looked at her children once again.

"No, I didn't," Emily denied.

"I didn't either," Mark shook his head.

Annie noticed how Craig and Sage exchanged a guilty look, "But you two did, didn't you?"

"Uh..." Craig looked at his older sister for help.

"We had a hunch," Sage told her.

"Trust the two nosey reporters to go snooping into moms and dad's affairs," Emily couldn't help but say with derision.

"We didn't know the whole story," Sage glared back at Emily before looking at Annie apologetically. "Mark and I were worried about you, mom."

"I appreciate and love how protective and caring you both are," Annie looked from Craig to Sage. "But you should've just come to me and not gone investigating this."

"We're sorry, mom," Sage apologized. "Craig and I were only trying to find a way for you to keep the house."

"I know you were," Annie gave them a small smile. "On that note, I think I'll go to bed. I have a big day tomorrow as it is my due day on deciding on the offer for the house."

"Do you mind if we look over the offer?" Mark asked her.

"Not at all, honey," Annie told him. "It would be nice to get another perspective on it. Besides, it is your home too."

"Is there any more cocoa in the pot?" Emily asked.

"There is still plenty," Annie nodded. "You'll have to heat it again." She stood up. "I'll see you all at breakfast tomorrow."

"Why don't we go for an early morning walk like we used to do?" Mark suggested.

"That sounds good," Annie agreed before leaning over and kissing him on the brow.

"Agh," Craig moaned. "I was going to sleep in."

"You don't have to join us," Sage told him, leaning up to receive her goodnight kiss from Annie.

"But it would be nice for all of us to do it," Annie urged him. "Besides, I think you owe me." She gave him a cheeky grin seeing the pained expression on his face, before giving him a big kiss on the head.

"Night, mommy." Emily hugged her mother. "Sleep tight."

"You too, my angel." Annie kissed Emily on the cheek before turning to leave the room, heading for a shower and then bed.

Chapter Six
TEMPTING FATE

Annie sat at the table at the coffee shop with her four children in the Key West airport, waiting for Emily's friend, who owned the new aircraft charter service to Manatee Bay. Her friend, Addi, was taking a special flight to fly the four of them to the island. Annie still couldn't believe she was almost home. She had been both excited and terrified to be going back to Manatee Bay after a twenty-eight-year absence. It had taken two weeks for her to pack up the last twenty-five years of her life with the help of her four children. All the things they wanted to keep were on the way to Manatee Bay. Annie's father was making room in one of the many storerooms at Manatee Bay Inn for her.

Annie looked around the airport, and her eyes caught the flights still to leave Key West that day. It wasn't too late for her to hop back on a plane to New York, and she'd toyed with that idea ever since they had stepped off the plane in Key West. The longer they waited for Emily's friend to show up, the more the idea started to take root in Annie's mind. It had not gone amiss on Annie that her kids had stuck to her like glue the entire day as if they knew she may bolt.

Annie was sitting between Sage and Craig, who kept looking at his phone and grinning like the Cheshire cat every time he got a message. Annie wondered who was putting that smile on her son's face. She also knew better than to pry into Craig's love life as she never got a straight answer about it from him.

"Mom, it's going to be okay." Sage put her hand over Annie's. "I also thought it was going to be strange to be in Manatee Bay without grandma. But what I realized when I first stepped inside the inn was that she wasn't gone. While her photos are hanging all over the inn, I felt as if she was there right beside me all the time."

"I'm okay, honey," Annie assured Sage. "I admit that I am dreading going home, but I'm sure it will be fine. Besides, I'll have my beautiful kids and father there."

"And Ollie," Emily told her.

"Who is Ollie?" Annie's brow furrowed.

"This big stray golden retriever Emily brought back to the inn the day before she left the island last summer," Craig told his mother. "He is awesome, and granddad said he's been trying to find Ollie's owner, but the house his chip is registered to is deserted."

"It seems as if Ollie's previous owners just abandoned him," Emily's eyes sparked with anger.

"Oh no, that's horrible," Annie said in despair. "How can anyone do that to a poor animal?"

"Not to worry, mom," Sage patted her hand. "Our big-hearted sister found him and brought him in from the cold."

"I think that granddad was secretly pleased Ollie came into his life," Craig said. "He and the dog are basically inseparable."

"Your granddad always loved dogs," Annie told them. "And I'm glad he's got some companionship. I know he was very lonely after grandma died, and then a few years after that, his chef and manager left to go to Germany."

"I know. I was so shocked to find out that Chef Gordon and his lovely wife Greta had left the inn. I thought they'd be there forever," Emily sighed. "It just goes to show you that nothing is designed to last forever."

A dark emotion flashed in her eyes, and Annie's heart went

out to her baby girl. Annie may like Nate, Emily's now ex-fiancé, but she was really mad at him for breaking Emily's heart. Emily had put on a brave face these past two weeks. But Annie knew she was struggling and had heard her crying a few times at night in her room during the weeks they had been packing up the house.

"Em, isn't your friend running late?" Craig asked his sister, glancing at the big clock on the coffee shop's wall. "She was supposed to meet up an hour ago."

"I'll go give her a call," Emily said, scraping back her chair as she pulled out her phone. "Be right back." She turned and walked out of the café, where the cell phone reception was spotty.

"Craig, don't be rude, honey." Annie looked at her handsome son with his deep rich brown hair and warm hazel eyes. "Emily's friend is doing us a big favor."

"Yes, but we could be boarding the ferry right now, and it is only a ninety-minute ride," Craig pointed out.

"She's a good friend of Emily's, Craig," Sage told him. "I think she needs a good friend right now."

"Yes, I agree with you, honey." Annie sighed. "I hate seeing Emily's usually sparkling eyes dulled by sadness."

※

Tom Howard rushed through the crowds glancing at the oversized clock on the wall. He knew he was late to help Addi out, but Tom had a boat that had come in at the last minute in need of repairs. He was the only one at the marina that could sign the boat in. Tom stepped around people who didn't seem to know where they were going when his phone rang. He pulled it out of his jacket pocket.

"Hey, sweetheart, I'm almost there," Tom assured Addi.

He listened to her instructions for a second, stopped, and looked around him. The minute he saw the petite blonde woman standing and looking around expectantly, his heart froze in his throat. Tom's mind spun trying to remember the name of the person he was supposed to be meeting.

"What was the name of the person I'm supposed to be meeting again?" Tom asked, unable to take his eyes off the young blonde woman a few feet away from him.

When Addi repeated the name, Tom felt his heart drop to his feet as his mind reeled. How did he not put it together before he'd volunteered to help out? The voice from the other end yanked him back to the present, making him realize how creepy he must look leering at the young woman.

"I think I see her," Tom said before saying goodbye and hanging up.

Before Tom could start walking to the blond woman, she spotted him. A smile split her beautiful face, lighting up her violet eyes. It took Tom everything he had not to turn tail and run as she was the splitting image of a woman he once knew. But before he had time to make an excuse or exercise any plans, she was in front of him.

"Hi, are you the pilot I'm looking for?" the young woman asked him. "Because you look like the man in the photo Addi Grimes showed me of her father."

"I..." Tom swallowed and cleared his throat. *Maybe it was just her and her husband he'd be taking to Manatee Bay*, he thought hopefully.

Tom glanced at her hand. There was no ring. *Boyfriend maybe?* "Sorry. Yes, I'm Tom."

"Hi," she said, "We've never had the chance to meet before, but I've heard so much about you."

"You're the best friend that I've heard so much about," Tom said, feeling foolish at having said that, but in his defense, he was in a state of shock. And this woman looked like... *No, Tom, we are not going there.* He cleared his throat and looked past her to where she'd been standing. "Do you have luggage?"

"Yes, but it's not here. Come and meet the rest of your passengers," she walked past him, giving him no option but to follow her.

Every instinct and nerve ending in Tom's body was screaming that his past was about to catch up with him and drag him under.

"Maybe we should go look for your sister?" Annie looked worriedly at the door.

"Mom, she'll be fine. You forget she knows this airport well. It's on her route," Sage reminded her mother. "I'm sure she'll..." She stopped talking as she saw her sister rush into the coffee shop. "There she is."

"Oh good," Annie sighed in relief and then nearly choked when a familiar tall, dark-haired figure followed Emily into the coffee shop.

No! Annie's eyes widened, and her breath caught in her throat as her heart stopped in her chest for a second. *Surely fate wouldn't be that cruel?*

"Mom," Emily called excitedly, rushing towards them. "Addi got delayed, but her father will be taking us to the island."

Addi's father? Annie's eyes flew up to meet the cool green eyes of none other than Tom Howard.

"Annie?" Tom said with a nod. His voice was level. The tone matching his cool eyes.

"Hello, Tom," Annie tried as hard as she could to keep her voice and demeanor just as cool as his. "I didn't know you were back in Manatee Bay."

"I moved back five years ago," Tom told her.

"You two know each other, mom?" Emily looked at Annie in surprise.

"Yes," Annie gave her daughter a small smile. "Grandpop used to be Mr. Howard's Hockey coach before he went pro."

"You're Tom Howard?" Craig's eyes widened in awe, and he stood up.

"Guilty," Tom said with a polite smile and held his hand out to Craig.

"This is my son Craig," Annie introduced him. "You've already met my youngest daughter, Emily."

Tom smiled at Emily before turning to look at Sage who was sitting next to Annie. Her protective instincts kicked in, and her hand reached out to grab her daughters.

"This is my eldest child, Sage." Annie gestured towards Sage, who merely nodded at Tom but didn't budge from Annie's side.

"Nice to meet you all," Tom said, glancing at his wristwatch. "We're going to have to get going. We've got an allotted take-off time that Addi has already had to move once."

"It's okay. I already spoke to the tower," Emily told him with a grin. "They've given us an extra fifteen minutes due to Addi's delay."

"That's great," Tom said, turning back to look at the luggage behind them. "I see you're all used to traveling."

"Yes," Craig answered for his family. "We're all in a line of work that takes us all over the place."

"Can I help you with your bags?" Tom looked at Annie.

"It's okay." Craig bent down and scooped up Annie's bag. "I've got it."

Before Tom could offer to take Sage's bag, she popped the handle out and stood up with her mother. Annie could feel the sudden tension between Sage and Tom. The twins had always been able to pick up on Annie's emotions, especially when she didn't care for someone. Right now, Annie knew Sage must be picking up on her tension. Annie's throat felt horribly dry, and little pricks of apprehension clawed their way up her spine.

"This way." Tom stepped back and let them all go out the door before him. "We have to go through the main terminal to hanger eight."

Tom walked a step behind them, herding them towards the hangar. As they walked, Craig and Emily asked him questions about his pro hockey days. Annie was thankful they were keeping Tom occupied while Sage walked quietly beside her. When they were seated in the plane, Tom invited Emily to copilot with him, much to her delight. Annie knew it was a dream of Emily's to open up her own charter flight service one day.

After a nerve-racking thirty minutes, they finally landed at the tiny Manatee Bay airport, which was more of an airstrip with an office next to it. Annie was so happy to see her father waiting for them. As soon as her feet touched the tarmac Annie rushed to greet him knowing it was a cowardly way to avoid having to speak to Tom. But Annie didn't care. She needed time to adjust to the fact that he was back on the island at the same time she was. A scenario she had dreaded for thirty-seven years.

"Hi, dad." Annie embraced her father but not too tightly. She was mindful of the brace he was still wearing on his injured arm. "How are you feeling?"

"The shoulder is a lot better," Jim told his daughter. "How was your flight?" He asked just before he got bombarded with greetings from his four grandchildren.

"It was fine," Annie lied. "I am exhausted, though, and I'm looking forward to a hot bath."

"If you've got everything, we'll just say goodbye to Tom and get going," Jim said, making Annie's heart sink.

The last thing she wanted to do was talk to Tom again. Annie wasn't even sure she wanted to stay on the island now that she knew he was back. But she'd committed to helping her father and spending the summer with him and her children. There was no backing out now, especially when the only way back to the mainland was either a ferry ride or the flight charter service owned by Tom and his daughter.

Driving towards the Manatee Bay Inn, Annie took in all the sights, marveling at how her small island hometown had grown. Empty spaces where she and her friends had played as children now either had shops, offices, or condominiums on them. Some of the old houses that used to line up the street leading up to the inn and Manatee Sanctuary had been pulled down or converted into businesses.

"What has happened to our neighborhood, dad?" Annie glanced over at her father in the driver's seat.

"There's been a lot of development in the area lately," Jim told his daughter. "Ocean side property in Florida is in demand these days."

"Which is strange considering climate change and the rising oceans," Craig piped up from the back seat of the inn's shuttle bus her father had fetched them in.

"I don't think the buyers think it is all that significant right now," Jim glanced at his grandson in the mirror. "It's all about being able to hit the warm beaches during summertime and enjoy a getaway to milder weather during cold city winters up north."

"I can understand that," Emily said. "I love New York, but I'm starting to prefer the milder winters these days."

"Old age getting to you there, Em?" Craig teased her and got rewarded with a punch on the arm.

"What have you been doing for a chef now that Gordon has gone, dad?" Annie asked her father.

"Oh, Carl from the Lobster Den and Lynn from the Ocean grill have taken turns to help out," Jim told her. "But as we've been closed for almost a year now, I've not had to have anyone cook."

"So, you've just been eating TV dinners?" Annie looked at him worriedly.

"What?" Jim looked at her with a pained expression on his face. "Good grief, no." He shuddered. "You know I would never do that. Your mother would haunt me, not to mention my mother. I cook a light meal or go eat with either Carl or Lynn."

"You said the renovations had started again, and the outside had almost been finished?" Annie couldn't wait to see her childhood home once again.

"Yes, I think you're going to get quite a shock when you see how I've upgraded the place," Jim warned her. "Your mother started modernizing it when you were here."

"And she never got to finish it," Annie said sadly. "I hate that she never got to spend her last few months at home."

"Honey, she had the best care she could get in New York," Jim assured her. "I was glad we all got to be together at the end. That is all your mother wanted because her home was where all of us were."

"I know." Annie cleared her throat and swiped at the stray tear staining her cheek. "I just wish we could have afforded the care she needed to be done here in her hometown."

"Well, it may be years later, but I've nearly finished completing the inn's upgrade and modernization," Jim glanced into the mirror. "My four grandchildren had a hand in the project as well."

"Oh?" Annie looked back at her children sitting. "I'm so proud of all of you for doing your part to help grandpops restore and upgrade our heritage home."

"Which we are about to pull up to," Craig pointed out the front windshield.

Annie turned and caught her breath as the majestic Cotswold-style mansion house suddenly loomed in front of her. It had been built by the first Williams, who had founded Manatee Bay Island and the house had been in their family for generations. The light brick of the house had a slight pinky-peach tinge to it, although her father always called it cream. The original house was four stories with a lower ground floor, ground floor, first floor, and second floor. It had been added to over the years with an eight-car garage off to the one side of the long sweeping drive that curved around to the front door of the inn. In the middle of the drive was an elegant water feature surrounded by her mother's beloved roses.

Annie smiled, thinking of all the gardening competitions her mother's roses had won. Bev Williams had loved to compete in the annual Florida flower festival. Annie had always been fascinated by her mother's passion for those flowers.

"I don't see a lot of changes, Dad," Annie said, climbing out of the van and looking around. "I do see you've kept mom's rose garden immaculate."

"That's what your mother would've wanted." Jim smiled. "And the changes are on the inside."

"Where is Queen Rose?" Annie asked her father. "Or is she no longer with us?"

"Oh, no!" Jim laughed. "I had strict instructions on how to care for our celebrity queen."

"Who is Queen Rose?" Craig asked, coming to stand in between his mother and grandfather.

"Not who," Jim said. "But what."

"Uh, oh," Annie teased her son. "Now you've done it."

"Once we've got you all settled in, I will take you to introduce you to our celebrity queen," Jim promised them mysteriously.

"Okay..." Craig gave Jim a peculiar sideways glance.

"Hey, little bro, stop goofing off and come help with the luggage" Sage said to Craig.

"Excuse me," Craig rolled his eyes and walked to the back of the van to help his sisters.

"It's good to have you home, Annie," Jim put his arm around her shoulders and gave her a squeeze. "It's been long overdue."

"I know, dad." Annie sighed. "I'm really glad to be home"

"I've put you in your old room in the house," Jim told her. "The kids are back in the rooms they used when they were little."

"Thank you, dad." Annie smiled up at him. "Now show me all these changes you claimed to have made. It does look like you've just had the roof and the stone sandblasted, though. It's pristine."

"Yes, it was getting a little old," Jim said. "Come. Let me show you the extensions and renovations."

While the children took the bags into the house and stashed them in the rooms, Jim took Annie around her old family home, showing her how much it had changed since she was there last.

Chapter Seven

ONE SURPRISE AFTER ANOTHER

Tom arrived back at the marina that bordered his sports shop. It had belonged to his parents when he was growing up. Tom's mother had been a professional ice skater that had won three gold medals before meeting his father. His father was a pro hockey player for the same team as Jim Williams, Annie's father. The reason Tom's parents had moved to Manatee Bay was Jim. He'd brought Tom's father, Greg, home to Manatee Bay after he'd been injured. Jim's father was an orthopedic surgeon. The man had helped Greg get back in the game for a few more years. But Greg had fallen in love with Manatee Bay. He returned home with Jim, who insisted on going home every Christmas, as often as he could.

Jim had introduced Greg Howard to his wife, Regina. Jim's wife was a ballet teacher, and she was helping Regina strengthen an injury with ballet. Greg and Regina fell in love on the small island of Manatee Bay. When Regina fell pregnant with Tom, his parents thought it would be the best place to raise their child. When the old marina and the attached fishing bait and tackle shop went up for sale, his parents had bought that place. The Howards had transformed the marina and the shop into what they were today: a major sports shop that sold the Howards' unique line of sports clothes, along with sports equipment, including what the original shop sold — bait, tackle, and fishing items. And the Marina could now birth twenty yachts.

When Tom's father had passed away in a boating accident a year after Tom's mom died, Tom and Addi moved back to Manatee Bay. Here, he'd taken over his parents' business, adding a marine engineering center to it and a flight charter company in the past three years. They were also currently building a golf and yacht club while once again expanding the marina and old golf course that his father had built about twenty-five years ago.

Tom had thought he might miss living in a big city, having moved from Miami, where he'd owned a Marine Engineering Company. But he hadn't. Tom and Addi had thrived on the island. Addi had been born in the small Manatee Bay General hospital, and although Tom wasn't here the day she was born, as soon as he'd gotten the call about Addi, he'd rushed back to Manatee Bay. She'd become the light and joy of his and his wife's life.

Tom was not ashamed to say they had doted on Addi, and he knew he probably spoiled her, but he couldn't help it. Addi was the most special person in the world. She was kind, brave, intelligent beyond belief, and, much to his dismay, very adventurous. Tom had lost count of the number of times Addi's thirst for knowledge and adventure had nearly given him heart failure. Not to mention many nights at the hospital with her getting stitches, having a bone set, or being checked for concussions. Tom had tried to convince her to take up something thrilling like ballet or even ice skating. But Addi had already conquered those disciplines that she said were too tame for her and then asked him to buy her an ice bike.

Tom's mind switched to Emily, Annie's daughter. Addi had told him that Emily had been her adventure partner when they were at college. That is where the two of them had met. Tom hadn't realized who Emily was then and couldn't believe that the two of them had actually gone to college together. It was an incredibly small world, after all. Tom's mind went back to Annie. She had gotten even more beautiful with age and hadn't lost her flowing, graceful walk either. Now it made her look more regal. Tom shook himself from the thoughts of Annie. That was not a path he would ever venture on again.

"How did it go?" Addi's voice snapped him out of his musings.

Addi walked towards him, pulling the aviator sunglasses off her pretty face, and hooking them on the top of her coveralls next to their company's logo on the small breast pocket. Addi had long dark auburn hair scraped back in a flat round bun at the back of her head and shoved beneath a baseball cap she wore when flying the helicopter.

"Hi, pumpkin." Tom grinned at her. "I didn't drop them in the Atlantic if that's what you're worried about."

"I was wondering about that and why I hadn't heard from Em yet," Addi teased him, kissing him on the cheek in greeting. "Thank you for doing that for me. I know how busy you are right now."

"You know it's not a problem," Tom assured her. "How was your flight?"

Addi had been booked by a tech millionaire to fly him and some business colleagues around the Florida Keys, looking at real estate investment properties from an aerial view. He watched her as she took a clipboard off the wall and started writing on it.

"Tiring," Addi told him. "We really need to look into getting more pilots if we are going to keep expanding at the rate we are." She turned to look at Tom. "If we had even one more pilot, I could start advertising more flights. They'd have to have a commercial airline license as well, though."

"Did you say that your friend, Emily, flew commercial airplanes?" Tom asked.

He knew Addi had been hinting at offering Emily a job. Tom had even toyed with the idea but that was before he knew who Emily was.

"She does." Addi nodded in confirmation. "She also volunteers for the coast guard and flies their helicopters for sea rescue missions."

"Oh?" Tom looked impressed. "Then maybe you should speak to her?" He hoped he managed to muster some enthusiasm into his voice.

"Em works for a big airline flying short and long-haul flights all over America and the world," Addi reminded him. "I doubt she'd be interested in giving that all up for a dinky airplane charter company on tiny Manatee Bay."

"You did," Tom pointed out.

"Yes, because flying commercial airplanes was my stepping stone to owning my own charter company someday." Addi signed off the chart and handed it to Henry one of her ground crew members, who came to collect it.

"Have you asked her" Tom walked over to the refrigerator against the wall where they were standing.

"No." Addi shook her head. "But you may just have an excellent idea there."

"Of course, it is." Tom boasted, knowing full well Addi thought she'd just manipulated him into offering Emily the job by making it seem like it was his idea.

Tom took an apple and a bottle of water from the refrigerator. He held them out to Addi. "I'm not just a pretty face. I'm known for my ingenuity." He grinned.

"Of course, you are." Addi took the items and kissed his cheek once again. "Thanks, I have to go and check out the helicopter."

"Is something wrong?" Tom frowned.

"I'm not sure." Addi frowned. "I'll let you know when I've checked it out."

Tom watched Addi walk off, his chest bursting with pride. Not only had she become a commercial pilot, but she'd also gotten degrees in a broad spectrum of engineering, astronautics, and aeronautics. Addi didn't only want to be able to fly airplanes. She wanted to be able to understand them. When Tom had taught her how to drive, she'd insisted on learning everything about how engines worked, how cars were designed, right down to being able to change a tire. From an early age, Addi had exhibited signs of being an incredibly intelligent child. She'd even gone to the top school for gifted children in Miami.

Addi added to her already impressive list of degrees and knowledge like most women added clothes to their closet. When she was a teenager, and her peers were going on dates or pushing their boundaries of what it was to be a teenager, Addi was learning a new discipline or finding new adventures to go on. Tom and his wife had been worried about her missing out on her teenage years, but Addi would go into reasoning about teenage hormones and how they were better put to use by learning a martial art skill, or how to rock climb, or fuel the excitement of hurtling down the white water of an angry river in a dingy. He sighed and pulled a bottle of water out of the refrigerator for himself before going to see if he could lend a hand with the helicopter.

The small island airport had been part of the package from the air charter business he and Addi had bought. It was also right near the marina. Since they'd purchased the business, Tom and Addi had already expanded the aircraft hangers. The airport building would be renovated as soon as the office block behind it was completed. It was exciting times for Addi and Tom regarding their business. It was also a lot of hard work that couldn't afford him having any distractions right now. Which is why Tom could not let himself think about Annie Williams, or rather, Annie Davies, right now. Tom had to just make a point to stay out of her way and have as little contact as he could with her.

Is that why you suggested Addi ask Emily about working with them? An irritating voice in the back of his mind asked him. *So you didn't have to think about Annie or have any reminders of her around?*

Tom gave himself a mental shake and walked into the hangar, where he saw Addi talking with the aircraft maintenance man, Bradley Jones. They didn't see Tom as he walked up towards them.

"Are you sure about this?" Addi's brows were creased in a deep frown when Tom approached them.

"How else would you explain it then?" Bradley asked Addi. "Your passengers were just darn lucky that you're such an excellent pilot."

"What is going on?" Tom asked, a little alarmed over what he'd just heard.

"Hi, Tom," Bradley greeted him.

"There was a small problem with the helicopter, that's all." Addi tried to shrug it off, but Tom could see by the look on Bradley's face there was a lot more to the story.

"What was the problem, Bradley?" Tom decided to ask him instead.

"I think the craft was sabotaged," Bradley told Tom, ignoring the black look Addi shot his way. "And it is not the first time in the past month that this has happened."

"You're fired, Bradly," Addi hissed.

"Sure," Bradley nodded, knowing full well that he wasn't really fired. It wasn't a good week if Addi didn't fire him at least twice. "For this to go wrong just once, I may have thought it could've been something I overlooked." He shook his head. "Which in itself is not possible, but I go over these aircrafts with a fine-tooth comb. But four times in one month, Addi?" He looked at her with raised brows.

"Why anyone would want to try to knock me out of the sky." Addi rolled her eyes at him.

"Maybe they're after your millionaire admirer," Bradley suggested.

"He's a client, not an admirer," Addi corrected Bradley.

"I have to agree with Bradley on this one, Addi," Tom said.

"So, you agree that millionaire man Addi has been flying around Florida has a thing for her?" Bradley looked at Tom with a grin.

Tom knew Bradley was trying to lighten the mood as he knew how seriously Tom took any hint of sabotage. Bradley and Tom had been best friends since junior school along with their good friend, Sam Grimes. Sam had been killed in a motorbike accident. Tom and Bradley had thought it had been no accident. The police had insisted the brake lines on Sam's bike had snapped because they were corroded by rust. But neither Tom nor Bradley could find any evidence of rust on Sam's bike at all. They also both knew as a mechanic, Sam would never have let any vehicle of his get into a dangerous condition, especially when he drove his young child around.

"I've asked Jake Bellamy to come and have a look at it," Bradley told them. He raised his eyebrow at the black look Addi gave him. She didn't like Jake poking around on her aircraft. "Jake worked on fighter jets and other craft such as Apache attack helicopters in the military. He will know better than both of us because of his air force training."

"What is it with you and Jake Bellamy? I'm sure we can figure this out between us." Addi's eyes narrowed, glaring at Bradley. "So, he's a big shot aviation expert who happened to fly a few military aircraft in his day."

"You know, when you were a kid, you used to come for helicopter rides with me all over the bay when I was home on leave." Jake's voice had them all turning around to see him standing behind them.

Jake stood watching them with his arms folded across his broad, muscular chest, straining against his faded black t-shirt. His long legs were in torn washed denim jeans, and his feet were covered with well-worn Nike sneakers. Once Jake had retired from the air force, he'd put all his science degrees to good use by becoming a science teacher at the local high school. He was also the new high school football coach and helped Jim with the Manatee Bay Island conservation. He was the island do-gooder and jack of all trades.

"Jake," Tom greeted him, with a hand shake. "Thank you for coming."

"It's always a pleasure. I love tinkering around with aircraft," Jake admitted, greeting Tom and Bradley. "I was asked to look at possible sabotage of the helicopter?"

"You really didn't need to come. We have this covered." Addi said with a hint of scorn in her voice.

"It doesn't harm any to have another set of eyes take a look at the problem, though, does it?" Jake said in his science teacher voice that Tom knew irritated Addi immensely.

"Whatever," Addi said, annoyed.

Tom watched as Bradley and a reluctant Addi told Jake what had happened. Jake nodded and climbed up to look at the propellers. After a few minutes, he jumped down, took the cloth from Bradley to clean his hands, then walked over to where Tom was standing, followed by Addi and Bradley.

"I have to concur with Bradley on this one," Jake turned to look apologetically at Addi. "It could only have been sabotaged. I went over the helicopter myself last night." He looked up at Bradley when Addi looked surprised by his statement. "You've had a few near misses in the past month. I thought I'd take a look at the bird to make sure it was right for your flight today." He addressed Addi.

"Excuse me?" Tom stuttered. "A few near missus?" He turned his shocked stare on Addi. "You told me there was a slight malfunction with the navigation system."

"It wasn't slight, and it was no malfunction," Jake told Tom.

"This is why I didn't want *him* here," Addi glared at Bradley.

"Addi," Tom looked at her worriedly. "Maybe we need to ground all flights for a few days so Bradley and Jake can look over the crafts?"

"Are you kidding me?" Addi gaped at Tom wide-eyed. "No, absolutely not!" She shook her head emphatically. "Do you know the impact that will have on the business? And I'm not just talking financially."

"Honey..." Tom tried to reason with her.

"No!" Addi said, stubbornly. "For all we know it's Jake who's sabotaging the aircraft." She glared at Jake. "He was also trying to buy the charter business. Maybe he's trying to put us out of business so he can buy it for himself."

Jake sighed and looked at Addi patiently. "Addi, you know I'm glad that you and Tom bought the place. I only wanted to buy it so that the Ingles or their buddies the Carmichaels wouldn't," Jake told her. "It's bad enough they've been trying to tear down our heritage and turn our island into a tourist trap."

"Yes, they're trying to put up big fancy malls and resorts," Bradley said disgustedly. "If they'd gotten the only airstrip of the island, it would've given them carte blanche to expand their resort empire onto our little haven."

"Uh..." a female voice had them all turning towards the doorway. "Sorry to interrupt..."

Tom instantly froze when he and his heart did a flip when he saw Annie's facsimile walking towards them. He immediately looked past her to see if Annie was with him and felt oddly disappointed finding out she wasn't.

Chapter Eight
EVERY WHICH WAY YOU TURN

"*E*mily!" Addi's dark mood instantly lightened when she saw her good friend. She shot around Tom, rushing toward the blond woman who was just as petite as Addi was.

Tom watched Emily introduce Addi to her sister and brother. His brows creased as he noticed a look pass between Addi and Craig. Little warning bells started to ring in his head and his parental instincts went on high alert as they always did around guys who showed an interest in Addi. Tom reigned his thoughts in and gave himself another mental shake.

Good grief, seeing Annie again has me completely thrown. Tom drew in a breath to steady his jangled nerves. *Craig and Addi have just met. They are both attractive, of course they are going to eye each other admiringly.* Tom reasoned with himself, but he also made a mental note to keep an eye on Craig Davies. The man was far too good looking and roguish for Tom's liking.

Addi in turn introduced Emily, Sage, and Craig to Bradley and Jake. Tom's eyes narrowed as he looked at Sage. There was something so familiar about her – as if he'd seen her before. His frown deepened as he tried to remember if he had or not or if she just reminded him of someone. The thought buzzed at the back of his mind, and he knew it would stay there until he figured it out. Tom was also well aware that Sage had taken an instant dislike to him for some reason. That made Tom wonder if Sage knew about him and their mother's past history. An old familiar ache throbbed through his heart and pulled at his soul as he thought about that history.

"You've already met Tom," Addi said, drawing Tom from his thoughts.

"We did," Emily turned the full force of her smile on Tom, nearly making him stumble. She looked so much like her mother.

"We did, indeed," was all Tom could bring himself to say.

"So, you're Annie Williams kids?" Bradley grinned, welcoming Emily, Sage, and Craig to the island. "Sorry I meant Annie Davies."

"That's correct, also mom has gone back to Williams after the divorce," Emily answered Bradley. "It's nice to finally meet you, Bradley, Addi has told me a lot about you. She says you're the best aircraft engineer she's ever worked with."

Did I hear Emily right? Annie's divorced? Tom frowned wondering why Dianne hadn't mentioned that to him or if she even knew.

"Why thank you, Addi," Bradley beamed proudly. "Although I'm not sure how many other aircraft engineers she's worked with." He laughed.

"Oh, a few," Addi looked pointedly at Jake who just sighed once again and shook his head.

"Emily, you are the spitting image of your mother," Bradley told her. "Even if Addi hadn't told me who you were I would've known you were Annie's daughter."

"Thanks." Emily smiled. "I get that a lot, especially in Manatee Bay."

"I bet you do," Bradley said, his smile reaching his warm eyes.

"Did Addi say your last name was Bellamy?" Emily looked at an unusually quiet Jake. "Are you my mom's friend, Dianne's younger brother, she has told us about?"

"I am, indeed," Jake admitted, giving Emily a smile that Tom noted was forced.

Tom also noticed Jake's eyes darkened for a quick second as they met Sage's. Sage was giving Jake frosty glances as well. Tom wondered what was going on between the two of them and for some reason he had an almost fatherly urge to warn Jake away from Sage. He reasoned it was because Sage was Annie's daughter, Tom and Annie did have a history it was only natural he'd feel protective over her children. Even if their relationship didn't end on the best of terms, they had been very close once.

"How is your mother?" Bradley asked Emily, who was the only one talking out of her brother and sister who remained stiffly silent next to her.

"You could ask her yourself if you come to our barbecue tonight," Craig invited Bradley and Jake. "I'm sure my mother would be really happy to see you."

"Craig!" Sage hissed, giving her brother a warning glare. "You can't just go inviting people out this late in the day."

"We're not big on formalities here," Bradley assured Sage.

"Well, if you're not busy, you should definitely come." Emily also ignored the black look Sage gave her as she addressed both Bradley and Jake. "My grandfather has already invited half of his old friends as well."

"The more the merrier," Craig said, his glance sliding towards Addi, giving Tom that nagging feeling in his gut once again.

"We came here to look at your new business and invite you to the barbecue tonight at the inn." Emily turned back to Addi and then Tom. "You're both invited."

Tom gave Emily a tight smile and nod.

"I'm there," Addi said right away. "I was actually wondering what I would do for dinner." She looked at Tom. "Are you still going to Dianne's for dinner?"

"Yes," Tom said. "Although I'm sure Jim would've already invited her."

"I don't mean to interrupt your dinner plans," Emily looked at Tom. "But it would be such a nice surprise for my mother if you brought Dianne to the barbecue."

A smile touched Emily's lips and made her violet eyes sparkle so much like Annie's that Tom felt like someone had punched him in the gut. It took everything he had not to double over breathlessly.

"That's a great idea!" Addi spun around and looked up at him with that look Tom could never say no to. It had got her a puppy, a meerkat, and a few cats, and they had adopted a hippo at a wildlife sanctuary.

"I'll speak to Dianne," Tom promised. "Although Jim probably already invited Dianne. I did get a call from her earlier but have not been able to get her on the. phone. I think she's tending to the manatees at Manatee Cove. The reception is next to none."

Tom's eyes shifted to collide with a pair of jewel green narrowed ones. Tom felt as if Sage was warning him not to go to the barbecue. The old anger started to spark inside him once again. Tom didn't like being warned away and wouldn't take that from anyone ever again. Tom folded his arms across his chest and slightly widened his stance. He held Sage's glare for a few seconds before relaxing his features and looking at Emily.

"You know what, I also think it's a brilliant idea," Tom said, smiling down at Emily. "I'm sure Dianne will be so excited to see Annie again. They haven't seen each other in years."

"I think she'd really like that, and she needs her friends right now." Emily's eyes shadowed over for a few seconds. "What with the divorce and all."

"Emily!" Sage hissed at her sister once again. "Not everyone in the world needs to know about our parents' divorce."

"Let me show you all around," Addi said, breaking up the sudden tension that filled the room. She started to usher her friends away from Tom, Bradley, and Jake.

"I never in a million years thought that Roger Davies would divorce Annie," Bradley said Roger's name with distaste. "That man was a snake."

Bradley stepped beside Tom to watch Addi take the Davies family through to another hangar.

"Maybe Annie wizened up to Roger's underhanded tactics at

last." Jake stepped up on Tom's other side. "I wonder if Dianne knows about the divorce, because she didn't mention anything." He glanced at his wristwatch. "I have my last science class tomorrow before the holidays. I'll come by afterward to help with the helicopter repairs."

"Thanks," Tom shook his hand. "I hope you're coming to the barbecue tonight. I think Sage has it in for me for some reason as she only ever glares at me."

"I wouldn't worry about it too much," There was an unusual catch in Jake's voice, and something flashed in his eyes. Before Tom could fathom what it was Jake said his goodbyes and left.

"I'd better get back to work" Bradley said. "But Tom, if you can get Addi to suspend flights, even just for tomorrow." There was worry in his eyes. "We need to check all the aircraft thoroughly."

"I'll do my best." Tom sighed, knowing that Addi would fight him on that.

Tom watched Bradley walk off, and his mind went back to the shock of hearing Annie was getting a divorce. Like Jake, Tom also wondered if Dianne knew about it. He made a mental note to ask. Tom pulled out his phone to give Dianne a call to let her know about the barbecue.

Tom would bet his bottom dollar that while Annie would be delighted to see Dianne, she would not be happy about seeing him there. He didn't even know what had made him challenge Sage by agreeing to go to it. Since landing the plane that had brought Annie and her children back to Manatee Bay, Tom had found himself looking out for her. He was both looking forward to going to the barbeque and dreading it.

Chapter Nine
WELCOME HOME, ANNIE - PART ONE

Annie was tired and not in the mood for a barbecue, but her father was so excited about having her and his grandchildren home he'd invited nearly everyone he knew. That was basically everyone on the entire island of Manatee Bay. Hopefully, it excluded one particular resident on the island. Annie took a deep breath and looked at herself in the long mirror. The evening was quite warm, so she'd put on a pale blue sundress with small white daisies, and her feet were encased in flat strappy white sandals. Annie pulled a light blue pashmina around her shoulders and noticed her left hand. Annie had taken off her rings the night Roger had walked out of the door. Her hand felt so light and foreign still.

She'd put them back on the following day again, but that was mainly because it had become a habit after thirty-seven years. Annie had worn her rings for the next two days until her lawyer had called to tell her he'd received the divorce papers. That was the day Annie had taken her rings off for good and locked them away in her jewelry box. It still felt strange not wearing them, it made her feel lost and lonely. Now all that circled her finger were faint tan lines she'd gotten from all the gardening she did. This summer, Annie fully intended to make sure those marks were tanned over and gone just like her marriage was. Roger hadn't even waited until she'd sent back the final signed copy of the divorce to put a ring on Rochelle's finger.

For some reason, this had made Annie angrier than when she learnt about Roger's affair. Annie didn't know if their children knew about the engagement or not. So far, they hadn't said anything to Annie about it. She didn't want to add any more fuel to the flames. Annie took a deep breath as the anger started to boil inside her once again thinking about Roger wanting the New York Apartment. When Annie had her lawyer approach Roger's about it, Roger had been furious. He'd called Annie up and accused her of being petty and spiteful for going back on her word that he could have the New York apartment. Annie had been so shocked at first by the attack that she had been dumbfounded and couldn't find the words to say.

Annie had never said he could have that apartment. Roger knew that it now belonged to their children. Annie had merely consented to letting Roger stay in the apartment when he'd moved out of their house. She had told him he could stay there until he was back on his feet. She'd never agree to give him the place, and she wasn't sure where he'd gotten that idea from. Their children used it more than they did whenever they passed through New York City.

It was not more than a couple of hours after that conversation with Roger and him reminding her how he was struggling at the moment that Craig had sent her a picture of Roger. He was getting out of a brand new sporty convertible with Rochelle. Annie had called her lawyer to find out if he knew how Roger could afford a new sporty convertible car and the conversation she'd just had with Roger. Her lawyer told her to leave it with him and asked her if she knew her children had asked him to draw up an eviction notice for Roger and his girlfriend to vacate the New York apartment. It was the first Annie had heard about it no wonder he was so furious.

Annie frowned. *What is going on with him?* Roger had been flipping between a Dr. Jekyll and Mr. Hyde persona for the past three months. Annie knew one thing for sure though: Roger was no longer the man she'd grown up with or married anymore. What worried her and made her feel guilty was that she had noticed subtle changes in him over the past few years. She'd put these down to stress and pushed them to the back of her mind as she didn't want anything to upset hers or her children's idyllic life.

Good grief! Annie thought a terrible realization hit her. *Was I so busy focusing on the children that I neglected to see how unhappy Roger was? I refused to see it?* Annie closed her eyes and took a few deep breaths as giant waves of guilt crashed over her once again. Until that little voice at the back of her mind reminded her that Roger was the one that had lied and cheated on her. Annie had never lied to or cheated on him.

Annie pushed down the twisted ropes of emotions winding her insides into knots. She would take this summer to untangle them one by one. Even if it meant looking into the dark recesses of her life that she'd shut away because they caused too much guilt or pain.

Right now, she had a barbecue to get to. Annie had to put on her best smile and flow gracefully through the night which was being held in honor of her and her children coming home for the summer.

As Annie was about to leave her room, her phone rang.

"Hello," Annie answered.

"Hi Annie," Ben Carlton, her lawyer, greeted her. "Sorry to call you so late, but I have that information you asked me for about Roger. I thought you needed to know about it right away."

"I'm glad you called," Annie told him, turning to look out her bedroom window.

"I did some digging into Roger's affairs, and it turns out he managed to secure quite a substantial bank loan thanks to the sale of your Greenwich home," Ben told her, "Along with putting up a seaside property he owns in Florida, which he never listed in the divorce financial disclosure, as collateral for the loan."

"Excuse me?" Annie felt like she'd had a bucket of ice water thrown on her. "He owns a property in Florida?"

Annie's mind reeled. As far as she knew, Roger had not bought any property in Florida. The only property he had owned in the state, as far as Annie knew, was his parents home in Manatee Bay. Roger had inherited his family home when his father passed away three years ago.

"It's a house in Manatee Bay," Ben confirmed Annie's suspicions.

"I don't understand!" Annie felt tiny shock prickles tingling through her. "Roger sold that property almost two years ago." She frowned. "He even split the profits equally between our savings account and the children's trust funds."

"Did you ever check that any money was deposited by him?" Ben asked her. "Sorry, Annie, but as you know, I also handle your children's trust funds. The only money that has gone into them over the past five years is the money you've put in each month." Annie could hear Ben working on his computer. "Then the most recent substantial amount into their trusts was from the sale of your gallery and the portion of the Greenwich house sale."

"That can't be right." Annie breathed, her brow furrowing tighter, as confusion twirled through her. "Why on earth would Roger lie about something like that?"

"I have no idea," Ben said. "But if I had to guess, Annie, I hate to have to even say this, but it is possible he'd been thinking of getting a divorce back then already." She heard Ben's voice fill with compassion. "Why else would he lie about selling the place and then withholding the property from the divorce financial discovery?"

"I hate to even think he did something like that," Annie felt giddy.

"I can call his lawyer and demand an explanation," Ben assured her. "I could probably even get you the house in Florida because he'd failed to disclose it."

"No," Annie said, shaking her head and pinching the bridge of her nose. "I just want to put this all behind me. Let him have his house."

"But Annie..." Ben started to say.

"No, Ben. I appreciate the thought and know you're only looking out for me," Annie told him. "But let's leave it."

"Okay, but I am going to ask his lawyer about it," Ben warned her. "I'm sorry Annie, but you'll thank me for this."

"Sure, thank you for letting me know." Annie blew out a breath.

"I'll be in touch," Ben said. "Have a great time with your family."

Annie's head was spinning. *What is going on with you, Roger?* But before she could think any more about it there was a knock at her door and Sage popped her head in.

"Are you ready to go downstairs and meet the crowd?" Sage smiled at Annie.

Annie gathered herself and put on a brave smile, pushing all thoughts of her telephone conversation with Ben to the back of her mind. She'd deal with that troubling bit of information later. Annie walked to the door to follow Sage down to the party below. Pulling her bedroom door closed behind her, Annie looked over her eldest daughter. Sage was tall and statuesque with a long elegant neck. Her neat dark blonde shoulder-length hair swept softly around her beautiful face, framing her startling green eyes. This evening she was dressed in jeans, a cotton shirt with soft splashes of color, and sneakers.

"You look so nice and relaxed," Annie admired her daughter. "It's been so long since I've seen you so casually dressed."

"I'm going to take that as a compliment, so thank you." Sage put her arm around Annie's shoulders as they walked down the stairs together. "Did I mention that Emily invited her friend and father to the barbecue?"

Annie felt like she'd just been hit by a taser blast. The shock that zinged through her at hearing that was so strong it jolted her heart which started to hammer in her chest with force. Annie hoped that there were no more surprises in store for her that night because she wasn't sure she could take another one.

"Oh?" Annie did her best to keep her voice steady and

neutral. "Did they accept her invitation?" She didn't know why she'd felt compelled to ask that.

"Yes," Sage answered with a nod before pulling them both to stop halfway down the stairs. "And there is probably something else you should know..."

The doorbell rang. Annie smiled at Sage, "I better get that," she told her. "But hold that thought."

Annie turned to go answer the door and immediately wished she hadn't. She was greeted by her childhood best friend, Dianne Bellamy, now Dianne Reece. Although Annie was so pleased to see Dianne, her heart plummeted to her feet when she saw the man standing next to her.

"He's bringing a date," Sage whispered to Annie before greeting Dianne warmly, stiffly greeting Tom, and then going off to join her brother and sister outside.

Chapter Ten
WELCOME HOME, ANNIE - PART TWO

"*A*nnie!" Dianne's voice was filled with pure joy at seeing Annie. She immediately engulfed Annie in a big hug. "I have been waiting impatiently for two weeks to see you since your father told me you were coming home for the summer. Telephone conversations once or twice a month are not the same as physically meeting up."

"Hello, Di." Annie forced a smile onto her lips. "I'm so glad you could come tonight. It would not have been a welcome-home barbecue without you."

After Dianne stepped back, Annie was forced to look up into Tom's intense green stare.

"Good evening, Annie," Tom greeted her politely. "Thank you for inviting us tonight."

"Are you two going to stand blocking the doorway the entire night?" A woman's voice said from behind Tom. "Or can I please get through?"

"Oh, sorry," Tom stepped back. "Annie, this is Addi. Addi this is Annie, Emily's mother."

"Hi." Addi's warm brown eyes crinkled at the sides as a big smile split her lips. "It's so nice to finally meet you. I have heard so much about C... Emily's fantastic mother"

To Annie's surprise, Addi wrapped her arms around Annie in

a big hug before Annie had time to ponder on Addi's near slip of the tongue.

"It's lovely to finally meet you as well, Addi," Annie told her. "I too have heard so much about you."

"I'm sure we'll get to know each other over the summer," Addi promised before excusing herself to go find Emily out the back of the house by the barbecue.

"Your daughter is a lovely young woman," Annie tried to keep the stiffness from her voice as she looked up at Tom. "You must be very proud?"

"Oh, I'm extremely proud of her," Tom said, his eyes shining with his feelings for Addi.

"Speaking of children," Annie forced her gaze away from Tom to look at Dianne. "Why didn't you mention that Mark and Hannah were dating?"

Dianne's answer surprised her. "Because Mark asked me not to. He told me that he wanted to tell you."

"Yes, but he only told me a few weeks ago," Annie said.

"Excuse me," Tom said apologetically, breaking into their conversation. "I don't mean to be rude, but I think we should move onto the back patio as we are still blocking the front hallway."

"Oh, of course," Annie said with a small smile, feeling foolish that she hadn't even invited them in properly.

Instead, she was blocking their path into the house.

"May I take your coat, Di?" Tom smiled warmly down at Dianne. "Do you mind keeping the car keys in your purse as always?"

Annie's heart twinged realizing that Tom and Dianne really were on a date to her welcome home barbeque.

"Of course." Dianne turned and smiled at Tom, taking the keys from him.

The look between the two as their hands touched with the key exchange made Annie feel like she'd been punched in the stomach.

Stop being ridiculous, Annie. She admonished herself. *What do you care if Tom and Dianne are together?* Annie shook off all the tiny voices screaming in the back of her head and ignored the dull achy throb of her heart as an old scar deep within started to tear open. Annie took another deep breath to steady her frayed nerves, straightened her shoulders, and led her two guests to the back patio. They stepped through the double glass doors that led to the lawn that swept down to a private beach where the waves splashed onto the sandy shore. The big moon lit up the sky, showing off its sparkling array of jeweled stars while the ocean busily swayed back and forth, creating soothing sound effects in the background.

The warm salty sea air, the smell of barbecue, and people mulling around the garden reminded her of many other nights her parents had barbecues when she was young. She and Dianne would love to climb out her bedroom window to sit on the roof and watch from above while discussing everything. Annie and Dianne had still kept in contact over the years. They'd tried to visit as often as possible, which was hard considering Dianne and her late husband, Gavin Reece, lived in Tampa Bay. It had always saddened them that their children didn't grow up to be the best friends they'd always planned they would be. But it had been a nice surprise that Mark and Hannah had found each other.

"Can I get you ladies a drink?" Tom offered, his green eyes colliding with Annie's for a brief second before capturing Dianne's.

"Yes, please," Dianne said exaggeratedly, "I would love, love, a cold, crisp, dry white wine."

"Of course," Tom gave her another of his heart-stopping warm smiles that Annie could still remember so well after all this time. His eyes seemed to cool and turn polite as he glanced back at Annie. "What can I get for you, Annie?" His voice matched his eyes, cool, and polite.

"I'll have the same as Dianne, please," Annie gave him a tight smile.

"Oh, but put some ice in Annie's," Dianne lay her hand affectionately on Tom's arm and Annie felt the tear inside her rip a little more.

"So, this is new!" Annie observed, pointing to Dianne and then to Tom's retreating back once he was out of earshot. "You and Tom." She mustered up the most supportive smile she could and hoped that her eyes didn't betray what she was feeling inside.

That was really confusing for Annie because she got over Tom thirty-seven years ago.

"Uh..." Dianne looked a little awkward, "You know ... Uh..."

"Aunt Dianne." Sage took that moment to step between Annie and Dianne.

Annie did not miss the look of relief that swept over Dianne's face at the interruption. To Annie, that look was all she needed to confirm that Dianne and Tom were indeed dating. She knew that Dianne would keep it from Annie, waiting for the right time, because of Annie and Tom's past. That also led Annie to believe that Dianne may not be certain as to where her relationship with Tom was going or that it was quite a new development. Dianne used to do that all the time after they had been introduced to the world of dating for the first time in their teen years.

Dianne would date a guy, but she'd not make a big thing of it. Sometimes she'd even refuse to tell Annie who the guy was because she didn't want to jinx it or feel like a fool if it didn't work out. It was Dianne's way, and she was the biggest romantic Annie knew, so she let her best friend have her quirks. Dianne and Tom were also both single adults and had the right to date whom they pleased. Although she was itching to fish about it, Annie respected the fact that Dianne would speak to Annie about her relationship with Tom when she was ready to.

"So, how long has it been since we last saw each other?" Dianne asked Annie, drawing her from her thoughts making her realize that Sage had already left them.

"I think it was just over two years ago when you and Hannah came to New York for a marine biology conference," Annie recalled. "You and Hannah spent that weekend in Greenwich with us."

"That's right!" Dianne linked her arm through Annie's as they walked through the crowd that stopped to greet and welcome Annie back. "How are you holding up?"

"Better than I thought I would be." Annie started to fiddle with her now bare ring finger. "Confused and feeling a little guilty if I'm honest."

"Why on earth would you feel guilty?" Dianne asked her. "Roger is the one that cheated, lied, and cleared out your bank accounts." There was anger in Dianne's voice. Just like there had been when she'd spoken to Dianne over the phone about it a couple of months ago.

"Here you go, ladies," Tom came up behind them and Annie's heart instantly jolted.

Tom handed Dianne her glass of wine. When he handed Annie hers, their fingers brushed and a zap of electricity bolted through her arm, piercing her heart. Annie nearly dropped the glass of wine as she felt that tear that had started ripping earlier burst open.

You're just feeling vulnerable right now because of Roger. This means nothing. Annie forced her hand to steady as she pulled the glass away a little too suddenly, sloshing a bit of wine onto her sandals. "Oh, shoot, how clumsy of me."

"I'll get you a napkin," Tom's voice sounded a little gruff, drawing Annie's eyes to his. They were clouded with an emotion that was gone too quickly for Annie to identify.

"No, need." Annie mustered up a small laugh. "It will dry in no time as the evening is warm."

"If you're sure?" Tom gave her a tight smile then looked at Dianne. "If you don't mind, I'm going to join Jake and Bradley?"

"Of course, go ahead." Dianne linked her free hand through Annie's arm. "Annie and I are going to sit on the beach bench and catch up."

"Great, I'll leave you ladies to it." Tom gave them a nod and walked off.

"If we were in our teens." Dianne grinned as they walked towards the bench at the edge of the garden that bordered the sand where a bench dedicated to her mother was. "We'd be on the roof with our cushions and blankets under the stars." Her eyes narrowed. "We probably still could, you know?"

"Yes, but do you really think you and I should be climbing onto a roof through my bedroom window at our age?" Annie grinned back as the two of them turned to look back at the house where Annie's bedroom window was.

"Probably not." Dianne looked up at their old spot on the roof outside of Annie's bedroom window. "Although we are both still in pretty good shape."

"I was just about to tell you that you are still looking fabulous, Di," Annie complimented her friend. They turned to walk to the bench.

They sat down and a pain twinged her heart as she thought of her mother. The bench had been put in this spot because this is where her mother had loved to sit and watch the sea. Annie still missed her dreadfully. It would've been nice to have had her to talk to about Roger and his infidelity. Annie's mother seemed to have an infinite flow of words of wisdom.

Annie was about to kick her shoes off and dip her toes into the sand as she and Dianne started to relax, when she saw a red flare shoot into the night sky from the sea. Her brows furrowed, and she craned her neck to check if she could see where the flare came from, but clouds had chosen that moment to block out the bright moon. It wasn't long until she saw another flare go up and then a light flickering an S.O.S signal.

"Di, did you see that?" Annie craned her neck some more.

Annie put her glass of wine down on the bench and stood up to see if she could get a better view.

"I did," Dianne also put down her glass of wine to stand next to Annie at the edge of the sand looking out into the distance.

A third red flare shot up into the night ski and illuminated a yacht in the distance.

"I think it's a yacht in trouble." Annie squinted, trying to get a better look.

She and Dianne turned, sprinting up the lawn to find her father.

"Dad!" Annie called. "I think someone's in trouble out at sea." She beckoned for him to follow her as she ran back towards the beach.

Her father, Dianne, and most of the guests followed them, stopping behind Annie as she pointed to the faint signaling light tapping out and S.O.S coming from the sea.

"I'll get the sea rescue boat," Tom said from behind her, making Annie jump.

Annie turned towards him and nearly collided with him; he was so close behind her. She took a step back and her foot slipped off the small wedge from the grass to the sand. Annie nearly fell backwards, but Tom's hand shot out to stop her. That bolt of lightning once again zapped up her arm – only this time she saw some spark flash in Tom's as well. Annie decided not to think about what she'd seen. She stepped out of his hold.

"I'm coming with you," Annie said to Tom, who nodded.

"I'm coming too," Dianne told them. "And I think we'd better get moving. We don't know how long the boat's been out there."

"I'll get the helicopter ready just in case we need an airlift to the hospital," Emily popped up next to Tom.

"No, I don't think so," Bradley said, stopping her. "Let Tom go out on the boat."

"We're all going with him," Jake assured Emily.

"Let's move," Tom barked.

"I'll get the emergency services to meet you at the marina," Jim told Tom as the four of them rushed past him.

Annie, Dianne, and Jake followed Tom out of the front door to his SUV. It wasn't long before they were all piled onto Jake's boat that was used for sea rescue around the island and heading towards where they'd seen the distress signal coming from out at sea.

Chapter Eleven
NEW ARRIVALS

Annie wished she had stopped to grab her father's rain slicker on her way out the door. It was cold out on the ocean as the rescue boat bobbed across its surface on route to the stranded vessel. Even though they were inside a cabin where Tom was steering the boat, one door was open, allowing in the wind and some sea spray.

"There are some spare coats in the office at the back," Jake told Annie. "I'll go grab you and Dianne one."

"Thanks," Annie smiled gratefully at Jake.

"You're only here for a couple of hours, and already we're heading out on a high seas adventure," Dianne said, huddling closer to Annie as she was also cold, wearing only a cotton shirt and a skirt. "I should've gone with my instinct and put jeans on tonight."

"I was just thinking the same thing." Annie gave a shivery laugh, rubbing the tops of her arms.

"Here you go." Jake appeared, carrying two large rain slickers. "Like I thought, they will be way too big, but they will keep you warm."

"I don't care if they were giant size," Dianne said to her brother, grabbing the one slicker and pulling it over her head. "I'm not worried about what I look like right now."

"There!" Annie spotted the light that was putting out the S.O.S. signal.

"Heading there," Tom told her with a nod of thanks.

As they drew nearer, the spotlight at the front of the boat illuminated the luxury yacht, where a man stood waving on the deck as he saw them. Tom slowed down and maneuvered his boat around the side of the yacht. Annie noted it was called The Silver Fox. As they drew nearer, they saw a tall, extremely handsome man who was waving them down.

"Hello, I'm Finn St. James," Finn called up to them in a Posh British accent. "Thank goodness someone spotted our flares."

Tom had no sooner gained permission to board the yacht to help when a very regal-looking silver-haired woman popped up from below deck.

Finn St. James introduced the woman as Rose St. James, his mother. Her accent was even posher, as was her upper-crust posture and demeanor. The woman made Annie, Dianne, and Jake feel like they should bow or something when Tom helped her onto the rescue boat.

"Good evening," Rose greeted them.

"Good evening." Annie had to clear her throat and force herself not to curtsy instinctively. "I'm Annie Da.." She stopped herself. Annie had decided days ago that she was taking back her maiden name. "Annie Williams."

"Dianne Bellamy-Reece," Dianne introduced herself.

"I'm Jake Bellamy, and the man on your yacht is the captain of this boat, Tom Howard," Jake finished the introductions. "I'm sorry I don't have any tea, but I do have a hot flask of coffee in the back office."

"Thank you, young man," Rose addressed Jake. "Although tea is the drink of choice for most of my British peers, I must confess to enjoying my coffee more."

"I will get you a cup right away," Jake disappeared into the little cabin where he'd gone to get the rain slickers.

"Are you cold?" Annie asked Rose. "I think there may be some warm blankets on board."

"Thank you," Rose looked at Annie, and a warm smile spread across her lips, transforming the woman's face from stiff aristocrat to a mom-type figure. Annie was as taken aback by the transformation as Dianne was, she noted when they exchanged shocked glances. "But I have thermal undergarments on, about three cardigans, and my cloak."

"It is a beautiful cloak," Dianne commented on Rose's deep blue velvet faux fur-lined cloak that fell to the floor and covered Rose's feet. A faux fur-lined hood dipped down the back of the coat. "I also love your leather gloves too."

"Trust me, where I'm from, it gets bitterly cold, and these are essential items in any lady's wardrobe." Rose turned when Jake came back with a mug of coffee.

"I'm not sure if you like milk or sugar?" Jake handed Rose the mug. "But there was already milk in it."

"Thank you, I take milk, but I only take sugar in tea," Rose informed Jake, taking the mug. "We've had no power in the yacht for a few hours now. Finn thought he could fix whatever the problem was, but something or other got burnt out, leaving us stranded."

"Oh, no," Dianne said sympathetically. "You're in good hands with Tom. He's a marine engineer and knows everything there is to know about boats."

"That's a relief to know," Rose said, putting her free hand to her chest. "Is there somewhere I could perhaps sit down?" She almost spilled her coffee as the boat lurched over a wave. "I fear I'm not very steady on my feet at the moment."

"Of course." Jake stepped up to Rose's side and walked her to one of the bench seats in front of the cabin.

"Jake," Tom called him from the yacht.

"Yes?" Jake popped his head out of the open side door.

"Can you radio the rest of my rescue team and ask them to tow a yacht to the marina urgently, please?" Tom asked. "This yacht is not going anywhere on its own anytime soon."

"Aye, aye, captain," Jake saluted and popped back into the

cabin. "Excuse me, ladies." He pushed past Dianne and Annie to walk back into the office.

"How long do you think Jake's been waiting to say aye, aye, Captain?" Dianne shook her head as she watched her brother disappear into the office.

"I'd say since he was a kid and dressed up as a pirate," Annie remembered with a laugh.

"Yes, and he refused to take that outfit off for weeks," Dianne recalled. "My father had to bribe him to take it off just to bathe."

"Luckily, your father managed to distract him with a pilot's hat and wings" Annie reminded Dianne. "After that, it was all airplanes for Jake."

"And that made him follow in my father's footsteps to become a fighter pilot." Dianne sighed. "Much to my father's dismay, by the way. He worried all the time while Jake was in the air force."

"I can imagine," Annie said sympathetically, putting a supportive hand on her best friend's arm. "Emily signed up to volunteer with the coast guard for two years, and I found that nerve-racking enough."

"I remember you telling me that," Dianne said.

"Emily always wanted to fly. She was so disappointed when she realized she couldn't actually fly and had to learn to walk instead." Annie and Dianne laughed.

"Mom." Finn's large six-foot-two wide-shouldered frame filled the cabin as he stepped into it to carry two medium-sized suitcases. "I've brought you the bag you packed earlier."

"Why, thank you, my dear," Rose smiled at her son. "Finn, I'd like you to meet these two delightful ladies I've just met."

Rose introduced Finn, and Annie was struck by how handsome the man was. It was like he'd been perfectly chiseled by one of the world's best sculptors. Annie glanced at Rose. She must've been a heartbreaker in her day as she was still an incredibly beautiful woman who was aging gracefully. Annie tried to guess what age Rose was, considering Finn could be no more than fifty-two or three.

Not long after Finn boarded the boat, another vessel pulled up on the other side of the yacht from where they were.

"It seems my tow is here," Finn excused himself and ducked out of the cabin once again.

"Handsome fellow, isn't he?" Rose smiled knowingly at the looks she must have seen on Annie's and Dianne's faces.

"He is," Annie agreed. No sense in denying it that man was gorgeous.

But there was something in Finn's eyes that troubled Annie. Something deep and maybe even dangerous.

Almost two hours after they left on their rescue mission Tom pulled his boat back into its berth in his marina. Before Annie and Dianne could say a word to him, Tom was off the boat to supervise the berthing of the Silver Fox with Finn hot on his heels.

"Where were you headed before you got stranded at sea, Rose?" Annie asked her, helping her off the boat.

"We were on our way to Key West," Rose told Annie. "But it doesn't look like we're getting there anytime soon."

"That means you have nowhere to stay while your yacht is being repaired," Annie noted, and an idea popped into her head. "Why don't you and Finn come stay at my father's inn until your boat has been repaired."

"Are you sure?' Rose asked her, looking relieved. "Because that would save us a whole lot of trouble trying to find accommodation here..." She frowned, trying to look around for some sign of where they were. "Do you know I don't even know where we are?"

"Manatee Bay," Dianne told her. "It's a small island just off the coast of Key West."

"I can't remember hearing of it," Rose commented, looking around the marina which was lit by floodlights.

"Trust me, it is one of Florida's hidden secret gems," Annie assured her. "I'll call my father to get him to prepare two rooms for you and Finn."

"I hope it's not putting him out," Rose said.

"Not at all," Annie told her. "My father has one of the finest inns on the island. Only I must warn you that it is currently being renovated and repaired after last season's storm damage."

"Oh, I'm not worried as long as I have hot water to bathe in, a bed, and a roof over my head on solid ground." Rose sighed.

"Excuse me for a minute," Annie said, pulling her phone from her pocket and finding a quiet spot to call her father.

She'd organized with her father for their new guests and was about to go back to Rose and Dianne when she nearly ran right into Tom who had come up behind her.

"Oh, sorry!" Annie said, immediately stepping back out of Tom's hold after his hand had shot out to catch her.

"That's okay," Tom's voice was a bit throaty before he quickly cleared it. "I was coming to look for you to thank you for offering to put the St. James' up at the inn."

"I haven't lost all my small-town manners." Annie smiled at her joke.

"I never doubted you had," Tom said softly. "I'll take Dianne back to her house with Jake, and he'll fetch his car to come back to take you all back to the inn."

"No need," Annie told him quickly. "My father is bringing the inn's shuttle bus to fetch us."

"Oh!"

For a minute, Annie thought she saw disappointment flash in Tom's green eyes. "I'm sorry your father's barbecue was brought to such an abrupt end. I was looking forward to catching up with you."

"I..." Annie stood staring at him in shocked surprise, not having expected him to say that to her. "Well, maybe some other time," was all she could think to say, not knowing if she meant the words or not.

"I'll hold you to that," Tom said softly before Dianne walked up to join them.

"I see you found her," Dianne smiled at Tom and stopped beside him.

Annie suddenly felt uncomfortable, like she'd been cheating on Dianne by talking to Tom. *That's ridiculous!* She admonished herself. Annie had not done anything wrong by exchanging pleasantries with Tom. She and Tom had a history, they were allowed to exchange pleasantries.

That's not why you're feeling so guilty though, is it? Annie squashed down the niggly little voice at the back of her mind.

"I'd better go and get our guests ready," Annie excused herself. "My father said he was on his way."

Tom said nothing but stepped aside to let Annie pass so she could walk back to Rose. She didn't dare look back as she tried her best to hide how shaky her legs were from her encounter with Tom. While her insides were twisted in weird knots of confused emotions.

Chapter Twelve
ANNIE'S DEEPEST SECRET

Annie woke up with a start, sitting up straight in her bed. The sheets were twisted around her, and her heart was beating like she'd just finished a grueling dance session. She couldn't remember everything about the dream, but she could remember it had to do with both Tom and Roger. All she could remember was fog and being lost while she called out for help. Annie could also remember Tom shouting through the fog, *Remember, nothing is ever truly lost, and it can be found if you look or work hard enough to recover it,* in the dream. Annie couldn't remember the last time she'd had such a bad dream.

She glanced at the clock. It was two o'clock in the morning. Annie knew she wasn't going to be able to get back to sleep. She untangled herself from the twist of bed linen and hopped off the bed. Annie walked to her closet and pulled it open to retrieve her ballet training gear. She'd wanted to go and have a look at her dance studio which she hadn't gotten around to seeing yet. Her father said he had modernized it a bit and put a new sound system in. The building was soundproof, so she knew as long as she kept the windows closed and the music down, she wouldn't wake anyone in the inn or the house.

Once Annie was dressed, she padded softly down to the kitchen to grab a bottle of water and a clean towel from the linen closet. Nearing the kitchen, she stopped and frowned when she saw the light on and heard soft voices coming from inside the room. Annie walked in and found Sage, Craig, and Emily sitting around the kitchen table, having a discussion.

"None of you could sleep either?" Annie saw she'd startled them when they spun around and looked at her guiltily.

"Mom!" Sage's voice was filled with surprise.

Her eyes were drawn to Sage, who had immediately turned a document she was reading upside down on the table.

I wonder what that's all about? Annie decided to ignore it and walked further into the kitchen.

"What are you doing up?" Craig asked her.

"I had a bad dream," Annie admitted walking towards the fridge. "What are you three up to?"

Annie pulled out two bottles of water and looked pointedly at the document Sage had her hand on, on the table. A cold feeling slithered up her spine as Annie saw an official stamp on the back of the document.

"Oh, nothing!" The three of them said at once, making Annie know it was something.

"Uh-huh!" Annie's eyes narrowed as she looked at them. "You know I've been your mother for a long time, right?" They all looked at her wide-eyed. "I can tell when something's up." She pulled up a chair next to Emily and sat down. "So out with it."

Annie looked at Sage with her penetrating stare that made her children feel like fish on a hook. Sage and Craig shifted uncomfortably in their chairs as her eyes slid between the two. Still, they didn't say a word. Then her eyes fell on Emily, who squirmed for a few seconds before blurting it out.

"Mark gave Sage a document that shows that dad adopted them!" Emily looked apologetically at her brother and sister who were now glaring at her.

"Why do you always crack beneath mom's stare?" Craig shook his head at his youngest sister.

"We knew you'd do this!" Sage hissed at Emily. "This is why we keep things from you."

"I'm sorry!" Emily said to them, sliding down in her chair.

Although Annie felt bad for having broken Emily's resolve, she was glad for the few minutes reprieve from Craig and Sage to get her shock under control. She and Roger had known that one day they would have to tell the twins the truth. But that day had been pushed further and further into the future as their lives went on. Each day that passed without bringing it up had made it fall deeper into the pile of one day we'll get to it.

Annie gestured to Sage to hand her the document she had. Sage reluctantly slid it over to her, still upside down. Annie turned it over and left it lying on the table. She stared down at it. Her heart thudded against her rib cage while that day Roger had brought this document to her sprung into her memory. It was the day she'd known for sure that her ex-husband wanted absolutely nothing to do with her or his children. He'd cut them out of his life as coldly and callously as he had cut her from his heart when he'd sent her the annulment papers.

Annie took a mental breath and forced herself to keep calm. She was not going to think about that day or the dark painful ones that had followed it. This wasn't about her, it was about her children. Annie drew on the conversation she'd had in her mind with her children about this a million times over the years. *Stay calm Annie, tell the truth, but ask them what they want to know about the matter first.* She reminded herself of how she was going to approach this topic.

"Where did you find this document?" Annie asked, getting the conversation flowing.

"Don't be mad, okay?" Sage told her. "Do you remember when you asked Mark to make space in the loft in the New York apartment to store some of our stuff from the house?"

"Yes." Annie's mind started to go over what else might be stored there that her children could've found.

"Mark, found that document in one of dad's boxes." Sage pointed to the document now in front of Annie. "Mom, were you married before?" She glanced at the document. "Because the next two pages are mine and Mark's birth certificates, which list you as our mother..." She swallowed and glanced at the documents again. "But it lists..."

"Someone else as their biological father," Craig finished for his sister. "Someone who signed the papers, giving dad the right to adopt the twins." He glanced at the document. "But whoever it is, their name has been redacted." He looked at Annie excitedly. "Is he a super-secret spy?"

"Craig!" Sage rolled her eyes.

Annie blew out a breath. She knew it was time to tell her children the truth about her life before she married their father. But not here, in her father's kitchen. It somehow didn't feel right.

"How about we all go to the dance studio? We'll gather up some snacks, sit on pillows on the floor, and I will tell you what you want to know as well answer all your questions," Annie suggested. "I don't want to wake up grandpops."

Annie knew it was early hours of the morning, but she also knew that none of them would sleep until this was resolved.

"Done!" Sage was the first to say, scraping back her chair and springing into action to gather up some snacks. "Craig, why don't you go gather cushions and blankets. Emily, you help me with the snacks." She looked at Annie. "Do you want to go open up the studio in the meantime?"

Annie nodded and stood up. She picked up the document and walked out of the kitchen, taking it with her. Annie was glad she'd get a few moments to gather her thoughts before having one of the hardest conversations with her children she'd ever have.

An hour and a half later, Annie had finished telling her children the story of how her life had changed so drastically at the age of eighteen. Her throat felt raw from fighting back the tears, and her chest burned from the pain of reliving what was both the worst and best year of her life because she'd had the twins.

The morning was slowly breaking through the night as it started to light up the horizon, through the windows of the dance studio. Annie looked at her three children who were now gathering throw pillows, blankets, and the picnic basket. Sitting on the floor and telling her story was just like they used to do for family story time back in Greenwich when her children had been kids. They would gather in the lounge around the fire on the soft carpeted floor. Each of the children had a turn to choose what would be read for the night. Annie gave a nostalgic smile. At least that part of her life was stored as cherished memories in her heart, hers to take out at any time and happily reminisce over.

Annie knew, however, this story time was one of the hardest stories Annie had ever had to tell her children. All the other stories had happy endings; this one had an uncertain conclusion, because Annie wasn't sure what its outcome would be. Her part of the story may have been told, but there were still many other parts that had not, and some that were still to be written. Annie felt relieved and panicked, having finally revealed her darkest secret to her children. While her soul felt cleansed, her heart ached for how this affected them.

Although Annie had felt bad that Sage had woken Mark to join them over the phone, she was glad he'd also been a part of this. At least she would not have to tell this story a second time.

"You've always been my rock and the wise voice in my head guiding me, picking me up when I fell, and keeping me on the right path," Emily told her mother, standing with an arm loaded with cushions. "After hearing this, I think you are even more amazing than I ever thought." She walked over and kissed Annie on the cheek.

"When I was a teenager, I would listen to my friends' parents berating them and always pointing out their flaws." Craig rubbed one of his eyes, tiredly, balancing his share of items to take back to the house in his arms. "But you never did that. You were always so understanding and encouraging." He laughed. "But firm! You always used to say that we all have our flaws but then even the rarest jewels did."

"Thanks, mom," Sage said softly, kissing Annie's cheek. "It was a shock when I found out. I admit I felt hurt, angry, and betrayed at first. But then I realized that none of us had ever bothered to ask you about your life before we were born." She looked at Annie. "I know you were only protecting us from this."

"That's all a parent really wants," Annie told her. "To protect our kids from bearing the burden of our mistakes and troubles."

"While I'm still angry at dad for the way he lied to us, stole from, and cheated on you," Sage told her, "He took Mark and me on as his own children. Dad never ever treated us as anything other than his own flesh and blood."

"Yes, he loves you so much." Annie put her hand on her daughter's cheek. "You and your father were inseparable from the time you were born." She gave a small laugh. "He even bought an encyclopedia and whatever books he could to keep up with Mark."

"Yeah, I think most of us used dad's reference library to just be able to speak to our brainy bags brother," Craig reminisced and yawned. "Well, I'm going to get some sleep."

Craig kissed Annie on the cheek before saying goodnight and following Emily from the dance studio.

"Mom, I have to tell you something," Sage waited until Emily and Craig had left the room.

"What is it, honey?" Annie asked her.

"When Mark was leaving for university, he saw dad at the airport in New York with his new assistant and a small film crew," Sage explained. "He was going to the Bahamas to film something."

"Oh!" Annie said, surprised. "He must've gotten a new contract. I'm happy for him."

"Mom, Rochelle, was also there." Sage looked at Annie apologetically and bit her lip.

"Sweetheart, what is it?" Annie reached out and touched her daughter's arm.

"Rochelle was wearing an engagement ring," Sage said softly.

"Oh!" Annie's heart thudded heavily in her chest once again. *So, the children did know about Roger's engagement.* She blew out a breath, "Honey it's okay. Don't feel bad I did know about the engagement. I didn't say anything because it was your fathers news to tell you."

"He also phoned the day we left for Manatee Bay," Sage admitted. "He asked me to ensure that the boxes he'd left at the house got safely to Grandpop's house as well as the ones he was sending from the New York apartment's loft."

"Oh?" Annie frowned. "I believe he asked the same of Mark and Emily."

Why on earth would Roger ask about that so many times? Annie had already told him she would store his boxes with theirs at the inn. *Did he think I was going to throw them onto the side of the road?*

"Sage," Annie frowned at her daughter. "Did Mark tell you why he'd be going through your father's boxes to find this document?" She bent down and scooped it up from the floor.

"Mark was making space and saw a few of the boxes that were already stored up there open. He said it looked like someone had been rifling through them in a hurry as some of the contents were lying on the floor," Sage explained. "He was picking the stuff up when he saw that document."

"Mark, didn't open that box?" Annie's frown deepened.

Annie knew all the boxes that were stored in the loft in the New York apartment were sealed. She'd double checked them a few weeks before packing up the house as she'd arranged for the boxes to be moved from the apartment to Manatee Bay with the ones from the house in Greenwich.

"No, he didn't." Sage shook her head. "Mark definitely said the box was already open." Her eyes searched Annie's curiously. "You know Mark, he doesn't lie. He also said that wasn't the only box of dad's that had been opened. Once he'd tidied up the mess, he resealed them." She wrung her hands. "The only thing he took from them was the document you found us with tonight."

"That is so strange" Annie said. "I checked all the boxes up there before the week Mark stayed there and they were sealed, ready to be moved."

"Yes, I also saw that they were sealed before then," Sage confirmed. "I was looking for the box with all of Craig's comics in it as he wanted to make sure it was still there." She looked at Annie worriedly. "But I never opened any of them. I didn't have to because you are so thorough in marking everything that gets packed in storage."

"Did Craig or Emily say they'd opened any of the boxes?" Annie asked worriedly.

"Neither of them were at the apartment before we came here," Sage pointed out. "But I guess we could ask them?"

"How odd!" Annie said thoughtfully with a worried frown.

"Maybe it was just dad going through the boxes?" Sage suggested.

"When would he have done that though?" Annie bit her lip. "Your father had moved out a few days before Mark went back to New York." She looked at Sage questioningly. "Did Mark say your father had gone back to the apartment after he'd moved out?"

"Not to me, he didn't." Sage shook her head. "But I'll ask him."

"Thank you, honey." Annie smiled at her daughter who stifled a yawn. "I'm sure there is a logical explanation for this. Now you go and get some sleep."

"I doubt I'll be able to sleep after this," Sage said, stifling yet another yawn. "But I will go try while I'm mulling this all over in my head."

"You do that, honey," Annie told her. "I'm here if you want to ask any other questions."

"Oh!" Sage looked at Annie then glanced at the document. "There is one more thing."

"What is it, sweetheart?" Annie smiled at Sage.

"You've told us everything except who your ex-husband was." Sage's brow furrowed and she glanced at the document Annie had put on the piano. "That document has his name neatly redacted with a permanent marker."

Annie swallowed. Roger and she had agreed to tell the twins they were adopted but had made a pact to not tell them who their father was unless they really wanted to know. Annie was actually the one who'd insisted on it. She never wanted them to feel rejected by the man twice if they ever tried to contact him. Annie and Roger had taken a permanent marker and redacted the man's name from their birth certificates. To some it might seem a really silly or even petty thing to do, but Annie knew how the man's rejection had cut through her like a red hot blade. Her protective instincts wanted to protect her babies from ever experiencing that pain.

"Honey..." Annie swallowed. "I..."

"It's okay, mom," Sage surprised her by saying. "I have a lot to mull over right now. I think I understand why you and dad would redact his name."

"It was to protect you and your brother," Annie explained. "When Roger took the adoption papers to him to sign, Roger said the man didn't even blink an eye. He just signed you both off without a second thought and I never wanted either of you to try contact him and feel that pain."

Annie immediately regretted saying what she did as she saw the pain darken her daughter's eyes. The exact kind of pain she was trying to protect her from.

"I'm so sorry, Sage," Annie breathed and stepped up to her daughter, taking both her forearms in her hands. "I..."

"Mom, it's okay," Sage's voice was hoarse with emotion. "I needed to hear that, and I think so does Mark." She assured her mother. "It makes me not want to know who he is, and I'm thankful that I had Roger as my father. He may have made his mistakes now, but when we were growing up, he never once let us down."

"If Roger got one thing right, it was that he was a great dad!" Annie agreed with her daughter.

"I'm going to go to bed." Sage kissed Annie's cheek once again. Her eyes slid to the document on the piano. "Do you want me to take that with me?"

"No," Annie shook her head. "I think it's caused enough trouble for one night. I'll keep it safe with me." She smiled at Sage. Before her daughter walked out of the studio, Annie reminded her, "Sage, please remember that your grandfather doesn't know about the adoption. As far as he and your grandmother knew, you were Roger's children."

"We won't say anything to grandpops," Sage promised. "Night, mom." She turned and left the dance studio.

Chapter Thirteen
NO TRUTH STAYS BURIED FOREVER - PART ONE

*A*nnie stood staring at the empty studio doorway her children had just exited from. Her heart was hammering in overdrive. She was so relieved that the conversation was finally over and done with. The truth was out, and Annie knew there would still be a lot of questions her children would come back with. Especially Mark, after he'd mulled it over for a while. The one she dreaded answering the most was who their biological father was. Annie wasn't even sure if she had a right to tell them, because the man clearly didn't want anything to do with them. It was almost as if he didn't believe they were his children. Especially by the way Roger had described the conversation he had had with the man when he'd approached him to get him to sign the adoption papers.

The twins biological father hadn't even flinched or batted eye when he'd seen Sage recently and he must've known Sage was his daughter. Annie once again felt like she'd started to bleed on the inside, having relived the story. She'd been so surprised at how raw that old wound still was after all these years, but she guessed she shouldn't have been that surprised after the night before. She turned and looked around the room that had once been her haven. The place she'd come to every single day as often as she could to dance. But back then she'd come to dance with joy in her heart for her art. Ballet had been – and if she was honest, still was – her passion and was once going to be her career.

Annie turned and walked through to the dressing room that was off to the one side of the studio. It was a room that had a nice day bed in it, two dressing tables, and cupboards that held her ballet clothes and shoes. The one side also held her favorite dance music, photos of her ballet progression, and proof of all the ballet shows she'd performed. There was also a full bathroom off to the side of the dressing room and a small kitchenette.

Her eyes fell on the bed and frowned. It looked a little rumpled, like someone had been sleeping on it and carelessly pulled the comforter up in a hurry to make it look like the bed had been made.

Maybe dad took a nap there? Annie thought with a smile. He did that at times. She ignored the rumpled bed, padded over to the closet that held her ballet slippers, and opened it. Annie grinned when she saw all her old pointe shoes. She knew they'd still fit her as her feet were still the same size as they were when she was eighteen. Her father had kept them in good condition. Annie pulled out her favorite pair.

"Hello, old friends," Annie said to them.

Annie went back to the dance floor and over to the piano, where she'd put her phone next to that horrible adoption document. She turned the document over. Annie really didn't want to have to see it again. She hooked her phone up to the sound system, scrolling through her music selection to find the piece she wanted. After she had it ready, she sat on the floor, kicked off her shoes and put her pointe shoes on. She walked over to the bar and glanced around the room. Her father had told her he'd upgraded the studio with a mind to making it into a dance school for aspiring young ballet dancers in honor of Annie's mother. Annie was very much in favor of that idea. This studio needed to come back to life to inspire other young dancers as it had her.

Over the years, Annie kept up with her ballet dancing, but it was mainly to keep in shape at a local dance studio she went to a few times a week. She also incorporated her stretching routine into her housework and gardening whenever she could. She warmed up for the next half an hour before attempting her favorite old routine. Annie's system was buzzing from the intense warm-up she'd put herself through, which had worked off some of her tension. Her heart fluttered as she took her position and waited for the music to build. Annie loved this part, the anticipated build up to the beginning of the dance. It always gave her that feeling of excitement you got in your stomach like a child on Christmas morning. She closed her eyes, breathing in the beat.

As soon as she took her first few steps into the routine, the world around her faded, and Annie became the character she was dancing. All her hurt, anger, disappointment, broken dreams, shattered heart, and ripped-apart soul poured passionately into the dance. Her muscle memory took over, and she gave all she had to the music. She played out the past thirty-seven years of her life in the different characters her dance routine took her through. Each move Annie made was flawless and effortless as if she still danced every day of her life. As the music and her mixed routine came to an end, Annie's mind was once again clear even though there was still a deep ache in her soul, she knew the worst was over. Not much more could go wrong in her life, right?

Annie was deep in thought as she scooped up her towel to dry herself off and walked over to turn off the sound system. It wasn't until she'd heard the clapping that she realized she was no longer alone in her dance studio. Annie whirled around, Freezing on the spot, her heart leaping into her throat when her blue eyes met the green ones of Tom.

"How long have you been standing there?" Annie looked at him accusingly.

"I'm so sorry, Annie. I came by to see you and saw the door to the studio open," Tom said apologetically. "When I heard the music and popped my head in, I couldn't disturb you." His eyes darkened. "You're still one of the most gorgeous dancers." His voice dropped.

"What the heck are you doing up here, Tom?" Annie's eyes narrowed. "It's about five in the morning."

"Actually, it's almost six, and I know you're usually an early riser," Tom told her. He walked towards her pulling a brown envelope from beneath his arm. "I was hoping to catch you on your own."

"Why?" Annie looked at him, her eyes sliding towards the document lying upside down on the piano.

She had to stop herself from making a dash towards it to try and somehow hide it from prying eyes.

"We need to talk," Tom said.

"What could we possibly have to talk about?" Annie couldn't stop the catch of bitterness that edged her voice while her eyes watched him take a step closer.

Annie saw Tom flinch as if she'd struck him, and her brow creased in further confusion when a look of pain sliced through his green eyes. But that was gone as quickly as it appeared. Tom had stopped a few feet in front of her and held out the envelope to her. Annie glanced down at it and then back up into his eyes. They were once again cool and aloof.

"This," Tom pushed the envelope towards her once again.

Annie's frown deepened as she looked at the brown envelope that had his name scrawled on it. A strange tingling sensation started to dance down her spine. She looked up at him questioningly.

"What is this?" Annie asked him, suddenly knowing that she wasn't going to like the answer.

"Open it," Tom instructed with a nod and held it out to her for a third time.

She looked back down at the envelope. Her heart started to thud when she cautiously reached out and took it, carefully avoiding any contact with him. She opened the unsealed flap to look inside before pulling the document out. Her breath caught in her throat, and her eyes widened in shock when she saw what she held in her hands.

"Why are you giving me this?" Annie asked him, her voice hoarse with pain at seeing the documents she had never wanted to see again.

Only there was something different about the document. It didn't look the same as the one she'd gotten thirty-seven years ago. Her eyes scanned the page and her breath whooshed from her lungs when she saw a big red *DENIED* stamped on hers and Tom's annulment papers.

"Is this your idea of a cruel joke?" Annie hissed, shoving the document back at him. "Isn't slapping me with these papers once enough for you?"

"My cruel joke?" Tom rasped, his brows furrowing angrily. Annie was taken aback by the burning emotion blazing in his jewel-green eyes as he snatched the papers back from her. "I didn't slap you with anything, Annie." The words sounded like they were being ripped from him. "This was all you, and now unfortunately, *your* little summer mistake has come back to bite us both!"

"Excuse me?" Something inside Annie started to wind up so tightly that she didn't know how much longer she could stand here going toe-to-toe with him before she snapped.

Annie and Tom had not spoken to each up until yesterday since the day annulment papers had arrived on her doorstep to be signed thirty-seven years ago. She hadn't had the chance to ask him all the questions that had clogged her confused mind upon receiving them. Annie had never been given the chance to find out what had happened in the few day's they had spent apart after arriving home from their honeymoon.

"You heard me." Tom's eyes narrowed, and his lip curled nastily. "But once again, you seem to be choosing to ignore me just like you did back then."

"What?" Annie said. His accusations felt like a punch in the stomach. *Did he really just lay the blame for what happened between us thirty-seven years ago on me?*

"Look," Tom said through clenched teeth, grating his free hand through his hair. Annie could see he was fighting to control the red hot flames flickering in his eyes. "Can we agree to put the past behind us so we can work together to get this sorted out before we find ourselves in a whole lot of trouble?"

"How could this have happened?" Annie nodded in agreement of the truce and looked at him confused. "Surely when I sent the signed copy back to you, you got it granted and filed?"

"What do you mean when you sent the signed copy back to me?" It was Tom's turn to look confused. "I was about to ask you the same question." His brow furrowed tightly. "I sent my signed copy of the annulment *you* initiated back to you!"

"I initiated?" Annie's eyes widened in astonishment. "What?" Her eyes went from wide to narrow, her brow creased, and her mind reeled. "Tom, I was packed and waiting for you to come fetch me when Greta brought me a brown envelope marked for my attention." Her voice wobbled as she was forced to recall that dreadful day for the second time in the past couple of hours. "You have no idea what it felt like to open it and find you petitioning for an annulment of our marriage."

Annie heard the rawness in her voice. She'd felt it with every word she'd just uttered that had seemed to scrape along the sides of her throat as they came out.

"What?" It was Tom's turn to look at her in astonishment. His face paled when her words sunk in. "I..."

Tom shook his head as if to clear it, squeezing his eyes shut, he pinched the bridge of his nose before opening them and looking down at her. The emotion she saw in his eyes nearly bowled Annie over. She felt her breath catch in her throat but once again the emotion in his eyes cleared as quick as it appeared. Tom was once again in control; in rigid control.

"How could you not have known that the petition for annulment had not been granted?" Annie asked him in astonishment. "It's not like you to be so careless."

Slowly, the numbing shock of seeing those annulment papers once again and then finding out the annulment had actually been denied started to wear off. A slow, hot anger started to curl up from the pit of her stomach. Tom's carelessness and want of a quick ending to their relationship all those years ago may just have landed them both in hot water.

Tom blew out a breath, "Annie, I ..."

Tom didn't get to finish his sentence when a voice at the door had them both spinning toward it.

"Mom!" Sage walked into the room, stopping when she noticed that her mother was not alone. "Oh!" Her eyes widened in surprise, then narrowed when she saw the looks on Annie's and Tom's faces.

"Sage, what are you doing here, honey?" Annie asked, just as her morning wake-up alarm on her phone went off.

The alarm gave Annie such a fright. She was all shaky when she went to switch it off. Her phone was on the piano and in her haste to get to the alarm, she accidently knocked the document next to it off. The paper fluttered to the floor. Just her luck it flipped face-up as it landed right by Tom's feet.

"I went to look for you in your room," Sage said, walking slowly into the room. "I had a question about the conversation we had earlier..."

As Sage spoke, Tom bent down before Annie could and scooped up the document on the floor. Annie didn't have time to snatch it away when she saw Tom's shoulders stiffen. His eyes scanned the document, and his face paled a little more.

"What is this?" Tom's eyes once again blazed, narrowing on Annie as he held it out for her to see.

Chapter Fourteen
NO TRUTH STAYS BURIED FOREVER - PART TWO

"Why would you even ask that?" Annie felt her anger rise, her blood started to boil, and her defenses went on high alert.

How callous could the man get? Annie stepped up to him and tapped her finger on the scrawl at the bottom of the page. A scrawl that Annie not only knew so well but had also come to hate.

"That's your signature, is it not?" Annie was so blinded by hurt and anger she'd forgotten that Sage was in the room.

"Him?" Sage bellowed, her voice jolting Annie from her fog of anger, she spun around toward her daughter.

Sage stood gaping up at Tom. Annie could see the myriad of emotions running through her daughter's eyes.

"Oh, Sage!" Annie breathed and reached out towards Sage.

"Don't!" Sage stepped back and closed her eyes for a few seconds.

Annie could see she was gathering herself. She knew her daughter well. Sage didn't like to display her emotions on her sleeve in front of strangers and Tom was a stranger to her.

"I..." Sage's eyes opened but they were shuttered. They fell on the other set of documents Tom had in his hand. She tilted her head and before Annie could stop her, she grabbed them from his hand. Sage's eyes widened when she saw what the papers were. "Mom!" She breathed. "Do you know what this means if this document is real?"

Annie looked at Sage's abrupt change in mood. It knocked Annie for a few seconds before what Sage had just read sunk in.

"Can you please explain this to me?" Tom finally spoke and held the document he'd picked up from the floor at Annie.

His face was a mask of stone, and his jaw was clenched so tight the muscle at the side ticked in overtime. Annie looked from Tom to Sage feeling like she was being attacked from both sides with a barrage of questions.

"I can explain it to you!" Sage's voice dripped with malice which shocked Annie as her daughter verbally pounced at Tom. "Thirty-seven years ago, you thought nothing about signing away your children." Her eyes narrowed and turned to chips of ice.

"No!" Tom shook his head, turning to stare blankly at Sage. "I have never seen this document before today, let alone signed it."

He looked at it again and frowned before looking back at Annie with a look she knew well. It was the look a parent got when they found out they were having a child. It was the look of disbelief and stunning shock. Annie knew that look well. She had not only seen that look before but had also felt it four times before. But that was also not the look of a man who had any knowledge that he had children. There was a look of genuine disbelief and surprise on Tom's face. It made Annie realize that Tom really may not have known about the twins.

But if Tom was telling the truth about the document, that would have to mean he either never knew what he was signing or that someone had forged his signature. Annie gave herself another mental shake and pushed the second scenario out of her mind. Tom must have been in a hurry and didn't know what he was signing. But even as Annie reasoned it out, she knew it was highly unlikely. Tom was very thorough with everything he signed, and that is why she was so amazed that he hadn't bothered to check the status of the annulment he'd filed.

Annie's eyes widened, her head shot around and she looked at the document still clutched in Sage's hand. Without thinking she snatched it back from her daughter and looked at it more thoroughly.

"This is not the document I signed!" Annie said, frowning as she stared down at the page.

"What do you mean?" Tom asked, stepping up next to her and looking at the document in her hand.

"This document states that the annulment was mutually petitioned between you and I," Annie pointed out. "The document I signed said it was petitioned by you."

"The document I got had the annulment being petitioned by you," Tom told her.

Their eyes met and held for a few brief seconds before Sage jumped into the conversation.

"Can I see that again please?" Sage asked, Annie nodded and handed it over to her. "Can I use your phone please, mom?"

Annie once again nodded and handed Sage her phone. Tom's words were swirling around in her brain and her heart was now pounding so loud that she felt breathless. Annie was so shocked by his words and the fact that she believed he had really only just found out about the adoption that words were currently failing her. She felt as if she'd been struck dumb and all she could do was nod.

"I'll take those," Sage said, not bothered that she was being rude when she snatched the other set of papers from Tom's hand before walking off towards the windows.

*

*T*om's mind was reeling, and his heart felt like it was pounding in his ears. He couldn't believe this was happening. It was like he was reliving the nightmare from thirty-seven years ago all over again. He'd gone home after rescuing the St. James' the night before to find the document on his doorstep waiting for him. Only this time, the nightmare had a cruel twist stamped with big red letters. Letters stating that the new life he'd built after he managed to put the pieces of his shattered world back together after Annie had been nothing but a lie. Tom had been so distracted by the big red denied stamped on the document he hadn't even noticed that the document was different to the one he'd actually signed.

Tom felt as if his chest was being constricted by a vice. Annie had not even been back on the island for a full twenty-four hours and already his world had been shattered to pieces. He swallowed as floods of emotions hit him all at once. Since meeting Sage something about her had niggled at the back of his mind. Now Tom felt like an absolute fool for not seeing it right away. He turned his head towards Sage, she reminded him of his older sister, Georgina, who had died of leukemia at the age of eighteen. Sage had the same willow figure, green eyes, and facial bone structure that Georgia had. Tom knew when his mother met Sage that she would instantly connect the dots because of how uncanny Sage's likeness to Georgia's was.

His eyes widened when the reality of it hit him. *Twins! I have twins!* Tom wondered what Sage's brother was like. *I wonder if he looks like me?* He had to drag his thoughts back to the current situations. Tom made a mental note to ask Annie about him... their son.

Tom and his late wife had wanted children, but they could never have any. His late wife had ovarian cancer and had to have her ovaries removed the second year of their marriage. The closest they had come to having a child was when Addi, at the age of five, became part of their family after Tom's best friend Sam died. Tom was Addi's legal guardian and she'd become the daughter he could never have. He loved her as if she was his own. Now he had three children! Tom felt like he had stepped into some surreal dream as the emotions once again started to hit him.

The strongest of those emotions was anger. Tom had been cheated out of the first half of their lives. He'd missed everything. Hearing their first cry as they came into the world and holding them for the first time. Their first tooth, step, words. The worst thing about it was he hadn't even known he'd had them until a few minutes ago. Tom hadn't even been given the opportunity to watch them grow from afar. He'd even been robbed of that. More anger spurted through him. Tom wanted to turn and blister Annie's ears about cheating him out of his children's lives when it dawned on him. She'd been just as angry at him for signing the adoption papers as he was at learning, he'd never signed such papers.

"Why did you think I'd signed the adoption papers?" Tom asked Annie.

"Because Roger met with you to tell you about the twins a few days after they were born to ask you if you'd be willing to let him adopt them as his own." Annie's eyes slid worriedly to Sage who was now examining the documents.

"I can honestly say that I have never met with Roger in my life," Tom assured her. "But I can tell you that the more I learn about the man, the less I like him."

Tom ran his hand through his hair, clenching his jaw while wondering where they went from here. All he did know was that Roger Davies had a lot of explaining to do and the man better have body guards when they did meet.

EPILOGUE

Sage had wondered at her peculiar reaction she'd had to Tom the moment she'd met him. It was as if she'd instinctively known him. If Sage was honest with herself, the minute she'd felt her mother stiffen when she'd seen Tom it had been in the back of her mind that he might be her father.

Sage was surprised at how remarkably well she thought she'd handled the situation. *This was going to be a fantastic summer!* She thought sarcastically.

Not only had she come face to face with the man who'd broken her heart last summer, but she also kept falling over him every way she turned. Now she's just met her biological father. Sage would've have loved to hate the man for signing them over to Roger Davies, the man she had called Father her whole life. But after learning Tom didn't even know Sage or Mark were his, had thrown her. She didn't quite know what to feel or where they went from here. What she did know was that she was once again furious with her adopted father. Not only had he lied, cheated, stolen, and broken her mother's heart he'd also basically kidnapped Sage and Mark.

Sage knew she should've rather taken her mother to a tropical island somewhere or maybe even on a cruise. Any one of those choices would have been a lot better than being stuck in the middle of this bubbling volcano of emotions that were being stirred up by decades of secrets, lies, and betrayal. And if she was right and what she suspected about these two documents were true, her mother and Tom were in for a world of trouble – by the look of things, trouble neither of them were to blame for.

"It looks like your signatures were traced onto both of these documents. Which by the way look like they are the original copies! As far as I know the originals should be filed away, and each party involved would've have copies of them." Sage looked back at her mother and Tom. "If you come here to the window, I'll show you."

Tom and Annie walked up to stand just behind Sage as she held up the annulment document.

"Can you see the hard outline around both your signatures?" Sage asked them shining the light on the pages as she held it up towards the sunlight now streaming in through the windows.

"Yes," Tom said. "You're saying that document is forged?"

"Not the entire document," Sage told him. "Look at the difference between these three signatures.

Sage shone the phone light over the two witnesses signatures and the presiding judges.

"Is that my mom's signature?" Annie's eyes widened seeing her mother's name on the page. "I didn't even see that. I was so astounded seeing it had been denied and that the document was different to the one I signed."

"That's my father's signature." Tom pointed to his father's signature as the second witness. "I don't remember your mother's or my father's name on the papers I received."

"No, they weren't on the ones I signed either and Greta was my witness," Annie told him.

Sage turned and looked at both of them, "Do you have your copies of those documents?"

"I do," Annie confirmed. "But they are in the boxes from the house and are not due to be delivered until Monday."

"Mine must be boxed in the attic of my house," Tom told her.

"I need to see both of them," Sage looked from Tom to her mom. "I suggest you go see this judge who denied your annulment as soon as possible. Or at least get some legal counsel on the matter."

"I agree." Tom looked at Annie. "But we need to take both our copies of this document along with this one when we do."

"I can only get mine once my boxes arrive," Annie told them. "They are currently in transit."

"Are the courts open today?" Sage asked. "Or do you know where Judge Hansen lives?"

"I'm not even sure if he is still alive!" Annie looked at Sage and Tom.

"He is," Tom assured them. "I know where he lives." He glanced at the document in Sage's hand. "I can take this to him later today if you want me to?"

"I think that is a great idea," Annie agreed. "I'll try and call Roger." Her eyes narrowed. "I need to know why he'd lie to me about you signing that paper and if he knows anything about the annulment."

Sage noted that her mother couldn't bring herself to say the adoption papers. She took them and held them up to the light.

"This page is the same," Sage told them and showed them the trace marks around Tom's signature. "I agree with Tom that he did not sign this document."

Sage turned and handed the papers back to her mother.

"Sage..." Annie took the papers.

"I have a lot to think about," Sage stopped her mother. "The two of you have a lot to sort out as well." She looked from Annie to Tom. "I think we need to clean this up one mess at a time and right now, you two need to sort that one as a priority." Sage pointed to the annulment papers. She looked at Annie. "And, mom, I think it's time you had a big talk with da–" She stopped and swallowed. "Your ex-husband because I think he just added fraud and kidnapping to the list of his crimes."

"Honey, you don't know–"

Before Annie could finish her sentence, Craig burst into the room.

"Mom!" Craig's anxious voice echoed back to them, drawing everyone's attention to him.

"What is it, honey?" Annie's heart lurched when she saw the look of panic in his eyes. "What happened?"

"It's dad," Craig said. "He's gone missing!"

THE SERIES CONTINUES

ARE YOU READY TO READ Manatee Bay: Hopes, book 2 of the Treasure Seeker Series?

To read the next book in this series, go to www.amazon.com/dp/B0B5577VSJ

ANNIE'S RECIPE BOOK

Annie's Caramel Meringue Pie

Ready in **50 minutes**
Serves **8 people**

TIPS

You can cut down baking time by using a store-bought ready make pie crust.
It is easier to cut butter and lard into pea sized lumps with a pastry blender.

INGREDIENTS

- 1 ½ cups All-purpose flour
- ½ cup Cornstarch
- 1 cup Brown sugar
- ½ tsp Cream of tartar
- ½ cup Dulce de leche sauce
- ½ tsp Salt
- 4 Eggs – medium sized
- 1 ¼ cups Unsalted butter
- ¼ cup Vegetable shortening or lard

- 2 cups Milk
- 2 tsp Vanilla extract
- 1 cup Refrigerated filtered water

PREPARATION

1. Preheat the oven to 450°F
2. Sieve all the flour and ½ tsp of the salt into a mixing bowl.
3. Cut in ¼ cup of shortening and ¼ cup of unsalted butter into the flour mixture. Working the shortening and butter into the flour until it is in pea sized crumbles.
4. Add 2 tbsp of the cold water, toss to combine the mixture until it starts to come together.
5. Gently knead and gather the pastry into a tight ball that holds together.
6. Sprinkle flour on a clean dry surface and roll the pastry into a 12-inch diameter circle.
7. Carefully place the pastry into a 9-inch buttered pie-dish. Gently push the crust along the bottom and sides of the dish. Trim the edges that hang over the edges.
8. Place aluminum foil over the pie dish and bake for 8 minutes. Once that is done remove the foil and brown the pie crust for a further 5 minutes or until golden brown. Remove the pie crust when done and leave to cool.
9. Turn the oven down to 325°.
10. Pour the milk into a sauce pan over a medium heat.
11. Stir ½ cup of sugar and ¼ cornstarch into the warm milk. Use a whisk to get rid of any lumps.
12. Slowly stir in the dulce de leche until the mixture starts to bubble and thicken.

13. Reduce heat to low and allow to cook for an extra 2 to 3 minutes stirring continuously before removing from the stove.
14. Separate 4 eggs putting egg whites in a mixing bowl and placing in the refrigerator for ten minutes. Place the yolks into a sauce pan.
15. Stir the dulce de leche mixture into the egg yolks and bring mixture to a slow boil stirring constantly.
16. Switch off the heat and add 1 tbsp butter, and 1 ½ tsp of vanilla extract to the mixture. Remove mixture from the stove.
17. In a small microwavable bowl, whisk together ½ cup of the water and 2 tsp cornstarch. Microwave 1 minute or until the mixture starts to boil.
18. Using the egg whites from the refrigerator add ½ tsp of cream tartar and 1 tsp vanilla extract.
19. Using a mixer on medium setting beat the egg white mixture until it has soft peaks.
20. Add 1 tbsp of sugar and beat the mixture for 1 minute. Repeat until ½ cup of sugar is used.
21. Slowly stir in the cornstarch mixture and beat until firm peaks form.
22. Pour the dulce de leche mixture into the pie shell and spread the stiffened meringue mixture over the top.
23. Use the back of a spoon or fork to swirl the meringue into peaks if they collapse.
24. Place the pie in the preheated oven and bake for 20 minutes. The meringue on top of the pie should be a nice golden brown.
25. Once the pie is baked remove from oven and allow it to cool for 1 hour.
26. This pie is best served after it's been chilled in the refrigerator for a further 3 to four hours.

Enjoy!

ALSO BY AMY RAFFERTY

To dive into your next read, go to https://www.amyraffertyauthor.com/

STAY UPDATED WITH ME

Thank you so much for purchasing or downloading my book! I am grateful to all my amazing readers.

To stay updated on all my latest books, newsletters, freebies and beautiful photos from the fabulous locations I write about, why not join my VIP group?

I will send you regular pictures of La Jolla Cove, San Diego and the Florida Gulf Beaches where I try to spend as much time as I can. I live in San Diego, my own 'Garden Of Eden' and I am in love with the sea and the beaches in the area. They inspire me to write lots of beachy mystery romance fiction to share with my awesome readers like you. To join me go to https://landing.mailerlite.com/webforms/landing/y6w2d2

You will be asked for your email. You also get a FREE BOOK whenever you sign-up!

FREE BOOK

To get your FREE copy of Cody Bay Inn Prequel - Nantucket Calling go to www.amazon.com/B0992NFTY1

ABOUT THE AUTHOR

Amazon #1 Best-Seller, Amy Rafferty is a contemporary romance author of feel-good beach romance reads with heartwarming stories embracing humor and love.

Born in New York, previously a Lawyer, she now lives in San Diego with her beautiful children and cats!

Aside from writing, publishing and running her home, she spends as much time as she can visiting the beautiful San Diego and Florida beaches where she has family and friends. She calls San Diego her 'Garden of Eden', inspiring her to write clean and wholesome romance novels incorporating mystery, suspense and adventures for her characters as they find a way to open their hearts and let true love in.

facebook.com/amyraffertyauthor
instagram.com/amyraffertyauthor

www.ingramcontent.com/pod-product-compliance
Lightning Source LLC
LaVergne TN
LVHW012026060526
838201LV00061B/4485